I SUDDENLY STRAIGHTENED AND DREW MY REVOLVER AND SAID, "HANDS UP!"

One of the guards in the back started up with his rifle. I shot him dead center in the chest, the power of the slug flipping him backward out of the saddle. I never paused to see the effect of my work, just swung straight on Gaines.

"Now, drop them rifles and get your hands up! DROP THEM, GOD DAMNIT!"

Wilcey and Chulo were scrambling out of the ditch, their rifles leveled on the party. Sawyer let his go. Gaines didn't have one, only his side-gun. But Ormsby had one on the wagon seat beside him. I told him to kick it overboard.

"What the hell you think you're doing, Wilson?" Ormsby said.

"Hell, I'm robbing you. What the hell does it look like, you dumb sonofabitch! And my name ain't just Wilson. It's Wilson Young!"

Other books by
GILES TIPPETTE

Fiction

THE BANK ROBBER
THE TROJAN COW
THE SURVIVALIST
THE SUNSHINE KILLERS
AUSTIN DAVIS
THE MERCENARIES
WILSON'S GOLD
WILSON'S LUCK

Nonfiction

THE BRAVE MEN
SATURDAY'S CHILDREN

WILSON'S CHOICE

Giles Tippette

A DELL/ELEANOR FRIEDE BOOK

*To Tommy Steiner,
who is my best friend*

AN ELEANOR FRIEDE BOOK

Published by
Dell Publishing Co., Inc.
1 Dag Hammarskjold Plaza
New York, New York 10017

Copyright © 1981 by Giles Tippette

All rights reserved.
No part of this book may be reproduced
or transmitted in any form or by any means,
electronic or mechanical, including photocopying,
recording, or by any information storage and retrieval system,
without the written permission of the Publisher,
except where permitted by law.

Dell ® TM 681510, Dell Publishing Co., Inc.

ISBN: 0-440-19518-7

Printed in the United States of America

First printing—April 1981

Chapter One

I hated to be coming back to Texas in such sorry shape, especially since I'd left there with so many high hopes after me and Wilcey and the Preacher had robbed the poker game in El Paso and made off with a pretty good chunk of money. We'd all been planning on using the stake to make new lives for ourselves in a new part of the country—California. For myself, I'd been wanted for so many years, and it had finally got so hot for me down on my home range down in the Texas border country, that I'd had no choice but to seek new pastures. My hope, as it had been for a number of years, had been to start a new life, start me a horse ranch, find me a good woman, and be done with banditry and the owl-hoot trail once and for all.

But it hadn't worked out that way. We'd each had $16,000 as our part of the swag we'd robbed out of that big poker game and it had seemed like all the money in the world, enough to last forever. Well, I don't know exactly how it happened that we ran through it. I guess it was like Wilcey was always saying, "That's the way it goes. First your money and then your clothes."

For me it had been whiskey and bad women and bad investments and gambling, and just plain stupidity. Gambling had done the Preacher in and I reckon it was as much that as anything that got Wilcey. Though he did go in partly on a horse ranch I was trying to buy up around Monterey. A year-long drought killed us on that.

But all that didn't matter. What did matter was that within eighteen months I was pulling a robbery again. And it wasn't long after that that Wilcey and the Preacher were joining right in again. And it wasn't too long after that that we were as wanted as we'd been in Texas.

So I'd figured, what the hell, might as well be hung on home territory.

That's how we came to be crossing the Texas border from New Mexico one night. We were more or less quartering north. My plan was to head for somewhere up in the Panhandle. I knew we couldn't go down to the border country. I'd been hot before, but I had an idea that that rich bunch of ranchers we'd robbed out of that poker game was still looking for us and probably would be looking for us the rest of our lives.

We made camp that night just above the little town of Lone Star, which is about halfway up the western side of the state. Well, we were a pretty grubby-looking bunch sitting around the camp fire that night—dirty, travel-worn, and broke. You'd never believe we were the same three gents who'd arrived in Sacramento two years before and commenced outfitting ourselves with the best that money could buy. Now about the only thing we had to recommend us was good horses and, in my case, the finest firearms money could buy.

But then as a man in the outlaw trade I'd always had a good horse and gun. Couldn't get by with any less.

But I'll tell you, I was getting just a little tired of the outlaw trade and wondering where it was all going to end. The worse thing about it was that I didn't have an idea in my head as to what we were going to do. We were so damn broke we couldn't have paid attention, and the area I was leading us into didn't have any fat banks or trains or poker games to rob.

Wilcey said, "What are we going to do, Will?"

All I could say was, "Beats the hell out of me."

We were all leaning back on our saddles, staring into the fire. Lone Star is in the plains part of Texas and it's flat as a billiard table and there ain't nothing in between the North Pole except a three-strand bobwire fence with the gap down. And even though it was just fall we could feel the chill in the air. Fortunately we had just enough whiskey left to sweeten our coffee and we were making out with that and the fire.

The Tinhorn said, "Hell, Will, we better think of something. It's coming on winter and is fixing to get as cold as a witch's titty."

The Tinhorn had been a gambler all his life before he had the misfortune to run into me and get into the robbing business and his style was hotels and frock coats. I could see where he felt a little worried about the plight we found ourselves in.

Wilcey, on the other hand, reminded me of Les Richter, my old partner, and Les had been the best man I'd ever known.

Of course I'd let him get killed.

I was getting tired of losing partners. I drained off the last of the coffee and whiskey in my cup and said, "Well, let's go to bed right now and then pull our freight for Tascosa in the morning."

I lay there in my blankets that night staring up at the sky and thinking, as I'd done so many times before, what a sorry mess I'd made of my life. Hell, here I was thirty-four years old, coming on thirty-five, and I didn't have a goddamn thing to show for it except the memory of all the men I'd killed as a weight on my conscience. Oh, sure, I was Wilson Young, and I was famous—in saloons and in whorehouses and places of that ilk. And I was known as a bad man with a gun, a man you didn't want to fool with; I was also known as a man who made a good friend, but a bad enemy. And I guess the few people who knew me best thought of me as a man who'd always keep his word and would never let a friend down.

Well, that wasn't much to show for all my years. As a matter of fact, other than making a living, I'd never really done all that much good at the outlaw trail. That $16,000 we'd taken out of the poker game had been the biggest haul I'd ever made and I've told you how long that lasted. And I didn't know why I'd never had any luck. Seemed that first one thing and then the other. Worst of it was I couldn't seem to get myself straightened out. If I'd wanted the owl-hoot trail I guess I wouldn't have minded so much. But it just seemed like circumstances and bad luck had sort of pushed me into the business and I'd never had any luck extracting myself.

But then I'd never had much luck of any kind. Especially with women. But, lying there, in that bald-ass prairie with that cold wind blowing, women, and what had gone with them, was the last thing I wanted to think about.

Across the fire I heard Wilcey stirring around in his blankets trying to get comfortable on the hard ground. It was funny how much Wilcey reminded me of Les Richter. Les and Tod, who were cousins, had been my first partners. In fact I'd grown up with them around Corpus Christi before the Civil War and before things just generally went to hell. They'd been in about the same shape as I had; their parents cheated out of their holdings by carpetbaggers and scalawags and we'd just sort of drifted into the holdup business together. Of course I'd lost them some years back when we'd robbed that bank in Uvalde. We'd lost Tod there, along with Chico and Howland

Thomas, and then Les had been killed later, after we'd separated, in Nuevo Laredo. I'd gone down there from where I was chasing that little senõrita in Sabinas Hidalgo to try and help him, but had gotten there too late and damn near got myself killed for my troubles. Would have, too, if it hadn't of been for three little old Mexican ladies who'd nursed me back to health in an adobe shack.

Not that Wilcey looked much like Les. They were both tall and lean, though both about thirty pounds lighter than my six foot, one hundred and eighty pounds, but they both had that sardonic grin and they both had that loose way of traveling. I guess it was partly that, that sense of humor, but it was more that sense about Wilcey that I knew I could depend on him in a tight that reminded me more of Les than anything else.

We'd met down in Sanderson, Texas, when he helped me get out of a fix with a couple of *hombres* who thought more of money than their lives and were intent on claiming that little money that was on my head.

Well, they'd paid for that mistake.

That was back when things had gotten so hot for me that I wasn't safe either in Texas or Mexico, so I'd been on the border just like a mugwump, waiting to jump to one side or the other, depending. I'd drifted into gambling then because I was trying to walk the straight and narrow and not call any attention to myself. I'd met the Tinhorn first, but hadn't paid him any mind until Wilcey and I had run up on him in El Paso where all three of us, unbeknownst to the others, had been heading to play in this once-a-year big stakes poker game that a bunch of local cattlemen held. Wilcey had known the Tinhorn before through gambling. Well, we'd all decided to throw our stakes in together and try to win a big chunk of money in that game. But when that had gone sour, we'd decided to rob it. Or, I should say, I decided to rob it, the others not having had any experience in that sort of thing.

But we'd brought it off and, in that little experience, Wilcey had proved to be a very steady man in a tight place.

The only thing that bothered me about him was his bitterness. But then I really couldn't blame him very much for that. Up until a few years back he'd had a pretty good-sized ranch up in the very part of the country we were heading for, the Panhandle, a good family, a pretty wife, and just about everything a man could want. But then his wife had run off with another man, taking the kids with her, and Wilcey had gone to pieces. Between drink and despair he'd managed to lose his ranch and just about everything else. He, like me, with nothing better to do, had drifted into gambling. But now, of course, he was worse off for, through my good help, he had drifted into the outlaw game and he really wasn't suited for it.

But the Tinhorn was even less suited for it. He didn't know much more about guns than a pig knew about formal parties and even less about being wanted and having to run and hide. He was so damn nervous when we'd pulled the poker-game robbery, I was more afraid of him having a gun than the people we were robbing. But he'd gotten through it. The worse thing about it was, after just what little experience he'd had, he'd come to think of himself as a gunhand.

And that can be very dangerous thinking for a man who doesn't know what he's doing.

We woke the next morning all stiff and cold from sleeping on the ground under what little cover we had. It was 1895 and we'd been hearing it was going to be a cold winter. We got a fire going and made some coffee and cooked a little bacon and sat around looking glum in the early morning light.

The Tinhorn said, "We got any whiskey left?"

I reached around behind me to where I'd left the bottle sitting against my saddle the night before. It was about half full. It was our last bottle. "Just this," I said. I leaned over and poured a little in each of their coffees and then sweetened mine a little.

We drank and ate, sitting silently. The Tinhorn poured himself some more coffee and then held his cup out to me. I put a ration of whiskey in it and he sat there sucking it up. He said, "Well, it ain't a suite in the Majestic Hotel in Fort Worth, but it does warm a body a bit."

Even looking grubby and dirty in a rider's clothes, instead of the frock hat and black suit he was used to, he still had a touch of elegance about him. I guess that's something that professional gamblers never really lose. The confusing thing was that Wilcey always called the Tinhorn "Preacher," for that was what he'd known him by in earlier days. It was me who had tagged him "the Tinhorn." He'd gotten his name, not from any religious convictions, but because when it came to showdown time in a poker hand the Tinhorn would raise his eyes to heaven and say something like, "Lord, smite my enemies. Give them busted flushes and bob-tailed straights and give me three of a kind." Or, "Lord, let me win because I need the money so bad."

Wilcey said, "Will, what you figure?"

I'd been dreading that question because the truth was I didn't have an answer. It had come good dawn and the wind was so cold you could damn near see the blue in it. Out beyond us our horses were stamping their feet at the end of their picket ropes and trying to make do with the dry bunchgrass that was about all the grazing that was available to them. All around us the countryside rolled on in endless, dry plains. I'd said the night before that we'd head for Tascosa, for I knew that to be the capital of the plains cattle country. But what were we going to do there to make a living was anybody's guess. I knew we had to do something and do it damn fast. We were damn near out of grub, about out of whiskey, and we'd fed the last of our grain to our horses two days before. And they wouldn't last on the poor pickings the country provided without grain.

"How much money we got between us?" I asked.

Wilcey said, "I got thirty dollars."

The Tinhorn said, "Maybe twenty."

"I got about that," I said. I looked off in the distance, holding my tin coffee cup between my hands for warmth, trying to think. Finally I looked over at Wilcey, "Well, this is your end of the country. What you figure?"

He shrugged. "Damned if I know, Will. Been a good many years since I been up here. I'm sorta out of touch with the situation."

I looked at him, wondering if it was going to bother him being on his home range. Wondering if the memories might not be too much. But he hadn't said a word when I'd first suggested it.

The Tinhorn said, "I know one thing, we damn well better move before we freeze to this spot. Goddamnit! What's the month, anyway?"

Wilcey said, "First of December."

The Tinhorn swore. "If it's this cold this early, what'll it be a month from now?"

I asked Wilcey, "Any ideas how we can earn a living?"

He shook his head. "Ranch work, I guess. I don't know what else is up here."

I snorted and jerked my head at the Tinhorn. "Can you see him doing that?" Or myself, I thought.

Wilcey said, "No, but I don't know what else we can do."

"Hell," I said, "let's saddle up." I stood up. "We'll head up toward Tascosa and see what luck brings."

We got away, trailing north, hunched in our saddles against the bite of the wind. The Tinhorn said, "Hell, I'd just as soon go down to the border country and be hung or shot as to stay up here and freeze to death."

"Now, now," Wilcey said dryly, "I'm told freezing to death is the best way to go. They say you get real warm toward the last."

"Oh, yeah," the Tinhorn said, "who the hell came back and told you about it?"

We kept going. Wilcey was singing, *"I don't know, but I been told, Eskimo pussy is mighty cold."*

We made a nooning, eating bacon again, and drinking coffee. They were still joking and kidding around, glad to be back in Texas, I guess, but my mood wasn't so good. I'd selected the Panhandle because it's about as cut off from the rest of Texas as you can get. That, plus there's damn little law in the country, it being as poor as it is, to feed just one cow. Oh, we could have gone to Arkansas or Missouri or some such, but we'd have been in the same shape. And Wilcey thought he might still have a few friends around that could help us.

As we trailed out that afternoon I figured we still had about a hundred miles to go and we'd need to push it. About the only good thing I knew about Tascosa was that Wilcey had said the last time he'd been there they had a bunch of saloons and needed more to accommodate all the thirsty cowhands that worked in the area.

We pushed hard all the balance of that day, made a cold camp that night, and then got off early. It was cold enough that the dew on the bunchgrass was frozen and our horses' hooves made a rustling sound as we rode through it. At noon Wilcey said we ought to raise Amarillo before too much later in the afternoon. "Country is starting to look familiar," he said.

I gazed all around and I was damned if it looked any different to me than it had the last several days. But it was his home range.

Later on that afternoon we raised Amarillo, it suddenly rising out of the prairie like a cow getting up in tall grass. It appeared to be a pretty good-sized town, maybe three or four thousand, but it was a pretty poor-looking place, weather-beaten buildings, some of them leaning a little. But I imagine it was pretty hard going to keep anything painted in all that wind and all those sandstorms.

"Let's get off the prairie for the night," I said. "We got to lay in some grub and grain for these horses."

"Yes, and whiskey for us," the Tinhorn said.

"I could use a little rest," Wilcey said.

I said, "We ain't really got the money for much high living, but we'll make out the best we can. We owe ourselves a little something. And if something don't turn up pretty soon it ain't going to make much difference if we're broke one day sooner."

We came cantering into town in good style, located us a stable, put our horses up, and then found us the cheapest hotel in town. We took one room and slung our saddles and blankets in there and then immediately decided to go and find the nearest saloon.

The streets were about as dusty as the prairie, but they did have boardwalks in front of most of the stores and we walked along them, our spurs clinging and jingling, glad to be back in a town. I said, looking at the dust in the streets, "I bet this place turns into a hog wallow when it rains."

"Don't have to worry about that," Wilcey said dryly. "It don't never rain."

We turned into the first saloon we come to. It was a

pretty nice-sized place with ten or twelve cowboys either at tables or bellied up to the bar. We took a table and ordered a bottle of whiskey and some glasses from the barkeep. When it came we poured out all around and then knocked them back for luck. Then I took off my hat, put my boots up on the nearest chair, and leaned back, letting the ache and chill run out of my bones. "Ah," I said, "that's some better." Outside that blue wind was whistling down the streets but, for the time being, we wouldn't have to get back out in it and that was good enough.

The Tinhorn poured out all around again and we sat, sipping slowly, enjoying it. Finally I said, "Ain't sure we got money for both whiskey and a bath. How ya'll vote?"

Wilcey said, "Shit! Have you lost your mind?"

We sat there for a time not saying much of anything. I wasn't feeling much danger of being recognized, not that far north, and it was a pretty good feeling to just sit there without worrying if some young buck was going to come up and want to know if I wasn't Wilson Young. A man can get awful tired of that sort of thing cause it generally means one of two things: Either it's some fool trying to get himself killed or else it means law. Either one is trouble. As we'd been passing through El Paso I learned that John Wesley Hardin had just been killed by a damn fool that had shot him in the back. Hardin had just gotten done serving eighteen years in the state penitentiary and was in a saloon, not bothering anybody, and this coward, trying to make himself a reputation, had bushwhacked him with his back turned.

Well, probably that will happen to every man that lives by the gun and I didn't figure I was going to be any exception, not unless I could find a way to get out of such a life. And, for the time being, I saw no way clear.

Finally I asked Wilcey how far he figured it was to Tascosa.

He said, "Well, if we get out in the morning we ought to hit there by mid-afternoon, depending on how the horses are feeling."

The Tinhorn said, "Why don't we lay over another day?"

Wilcey gave him a look. "Because we ain't got the money," he said.

I yawned. "That's about it. We going to need all we got once we get there until we can figure out what to do. I know we ain't got enough to gamble on. And I don't see no way we can do no robbing. This is about our last stand as far as avoiding the law. So we got to figure something out that won't call no attention to us nor get us wanted in this part of the country."

The Tinhorn said, "Say, Wilcey, ain't there any fat banks up in this part of the country we could take pretty easy?"

He said it mostly jesting, but I didn't like to hear him talk like that. I tell you the truth, the Tinhorn had started to worry me. You never saw a man so nervous in all your life as he was on that poker-game holdup but now, with a few more under his belt, he figured he was Jesse James. Wilcey just gave me a look and neither one of us said anything.

We finished that bottle then found a café and ate a good beefsteak with some potatoes and gravy and, for the first time, after eatin' nothing but bacon for five straight days, we felt like we'd had a meal. It was getting dark when we left the café and I'd just as soon have gone on back to the hotel and got a good night's sleep, but we decided to go back to the saloon and kill another bottle.

Wilcey said, "You don't know this country like I do, Will. What if we was to run into a dust storm tomorrow and us out there dry as toast? I tell you, a man can't be too careful in this country. Got to take precautions."

So we went on back over, feeling pretty good, and got us a table and set in to do a little drinking. The crowd had about doubled, but they were a pretty well-organized group and there wasn't too much noise or rowdyism. Well, we were about halfway down in the bottle when two men came in. One walked up to the bar, got a bottle from the bartender, and then hammered on the bar for attention.

"Gents!" he said loudly, "let me have your attention. Give me some quiet here. I got an announcement."

After a little the room got quiet and everybody turned around to look at the man at the bar. He was a well set-up fellow, a little older than me, I figured, and wearing good clothes. They were range clothes, but you could see they were of good quality and that he wasn't any ranch hand. The man with him had his back sort of to us so I didn't get a good look at him, but what I'd seen had been a sharp, hard-looking face with a set of eyes that sort of swept the room in a hurry. But there was no mistaking the two revolvers he was wearing at his belt. He'd taken off his coat and you could see them plain and I could tell he was a man who knew his business if guns were his business.

The man at the bar, when he had everyone's attention, said, "My name's Ormsby. I run the Skillet Ranch and I reckon most of you have heard of that. We're hiring men. We're paying a hundred a month and found. Any of you that are interested I'll be sitting at that table over in the corner for the next hour."

Then he and the man with him left the bar and went over and sat down at a table in the back corner. Ormsby sat up at the table. The other men sat right behind him.

Wilcey turned to me. "A hundred a month? If that's

the case, wages sure have gone up since I was here last."

"Does sound funny," I said. I rubbed my chin and took a look at the pair at the table.

I said, "Wonder what the deal is?"

The Tinhorn put in, "A hundred a month. What's that? That ain't no money."

I turned around and looked at him. He wasn't his usual dapper self with four days growth on his face and a dirty range-jacket on his back. "It's a hell of a lot," I said, "to hands that have been making forty a month. And you better remember we're flat broke right now. We ain't back in California paying that much for a suit of clothes. You better look in your pocket before you go to turning your nose up at a hundred a month."

We watched the table. For a while nobody went near it, waiting for somebody else to be first, I guessed. But finally a few started wandering over and then a few more. This Ormsby talked to them one at a time. Mostly he just shook his head and pointed at the next man in line. But once he did shake a man's hand, a well set-up cowboy wearing chaps and a good hat. Then he went into his pocket and peeled a bill off a roll and handed it to the man. The gent behind him, with the well set-up pair of revolvers, never showed a sign, just sat there watching. Well, I didn't know who he was, didn't know what his name was, but I knew what he was. Like they say, it takes one to know one.

Wilcey asked, "Reckon we ought to go over and look into this?"

"Let's watch a bit longer," I said.

We poured out and knocked them off for luck and Wilcey said, "You know where the Skillet Ranch is?"

"No."

He gave me that sardonic grin. "Right north of Tascosa. Biggest ranch in these parts."

WILSON'S CHOICE

"Hmmmm," I said, sipping at my whiskey.

Wilcey said, "Almost like they come to meet us."

"Yeah," I said, still watching the pair. They didn't have any company at the time, just sat there waiting. Finally I got to my feet. "Let's go see," I said to Wilcey. I pointed my finger at the Tinhorn. "You stay here and watch the bottle."

We wandered over. Ormsby and the man behind him raised their eyes as we came up. "Heard what you said," I told him. "Mind if we set down?"

He took a second looking us over, then nodded at the chairs. "No. Take a seat."

When we were down I said, "Well, we come over to find out what you had in mind."

"What I said." He was a businesslike-talking man. "Have you heard of the Skillet Ranch?"

I nodded. "Yeah, we know about it."

"Then you know we're a big outfit. We need riders. We're paying a hundred a month and found. All equipment and horses that you'll need."

I said, "That's pretty big wages for riders. Don't sound like you're hiring riders. Sounds like you're hiring guns. Am I wrong?"

He took a careful half minute looking me over. His eyes shifted to Wilcey then came back to me. "We expect the men we hire to know how to use a gun. We ain't saying they got to." He looked at us again. There was a bottle of whiskey sitting in the middle of the table along with several glasses. He said, "Care for a drink?"

"Don't mind if we do."

He poured out and pushed the glasses over to us. But he had one sitting in front of him that he'd made no move to touch. Wilcey and I let ours set too. Behind him that thin-faced man just sat there. He was wearing a flat-crowned hat pulled deep on his forehead. He never moved his head but his eyes kept switching back and forth.

I said, "You ain't explained yet what the work's all about."

He said, "What do you care? Wages is wages."

"I care," I said.

"All right." He sort of leaned forward. "If you know what the Skillet Ranch is, then you ought to know we control most of the cattle operation in the northern part of the Panhandle." He stopped and looked at us for a second, noticing we hadn't taken up our whiskey. He asked, "Something wrong with your drink?"

"No," I said, "we was wondering maybe was something wrong with yours."

He looked at us for a second, sort of half smiled, then picked up his tumbler and held it out.

I picked up mine. "Luck," I said.

Wilcey said, "Luck."

He said, "Luck."

And we knocked them back as befits the toast.

We kind of settled down and he said, "All right. The owners of the Skillet have been having some troubles with other folk's cattle. They've been having trouble with these latter day trail drives from the south, bringing cattle up with tick fever. The owners don't like that. Also, we've been having trouble with our own cattle drifting too far south in the winter. Then we have been having trouble with the local ranchers. And we've been having a good bit of trouble with cattle thieves. All of this don't sit well with the owners who've got a considerable amount of money invested. What they've determined to do is to build a fence clean across the Panhandle and thirty miles deep into New Mexico. A fence two hundred miles long."

He paused to let that sink in and I heard Wilcey give a kind of low whistle.

He went on. "They's a lot of folks don't like that fence. But it's damn near completed at a pretty big cost to the owners. They don't want that fence interfered with, if you understand what I mean."

He looked at me, but I didn't say anything.

"So," he said, "we're hiring riders to make sure that fence don't get bothered. We want it to stay just like we built it."

Wilcey said, "It's a drift fence, then?"

Ormsby nodded.

"So we ride fence," I said.

"You patrol fence," Ormsby said. "You do your job right and there shouldn't be any repair work to be done."

I rubbed my chin, feeling the stubble. "That's a lot of fence."

"We're going to have stations built fifteen miles apart. It'll just be a cabin with a horse corral for your remuda. But you'll be responsible for that fifteen miles. Once a month you come in to draw supplies and get your money. Then you get four days off. The regular ranch hands will fill in for you for those four days."

"Work alone?"

Ormsby shook his head. "No, that wouldn't be too smart. We're going to pair you up."

I jerked my chin at the hard-eyed man behind him. "Who's your friend there?"

Ormsby gave me a look. "That's Mister Gaines. Mister Joe Gaines. He's my assistant."

"Oh, yeah," I said, half-smiling. "What does he assist you with?" I looked straight at Gaines. He didn't blink.

Ormsby said, softly, "Whatever I want him to assist me with." Then he looked at me. "What might your name be?"

It was a fair question since I'd asked first. "Wilson," I said. I jerked my head at Wilcey. "This is my partner. His name is Dennis."

Ormsby looked at us a moment longer than glanced around at Gaines, who gave a bare nod. He came back to us. "Well, I'm going to offer you both a job if you want it."

"When would we start?" I asked him. I tell you the truth I felt damn strange. I hadn't had a job, or worked for wages, since I was a kid. And here I was talking to a man about going to work for him. I felt so out of place I didn't know if I was mutton or beef.

"Anytime. Go to the ranch headquarters, which is about forty-five miles north of here. Man named Bob Danning will put you to work if I'm not there."

Wilcey suddenly said, "This fence. How come you can just string that all the way across the Panhandle?"

"Because it's on Skillet land. We own three million acres up there."

But Wilcey said, "I heard a lot of that land up there is state land."

"Then you heard wrong," Ormsby said. "We either own it or we got it leased from the state."

I asked him, "Who you expecting the most trouble from?"

"Everybody," he said. "Probably more from the local ranchers. But we're tired of losing cattle to their roundups. We're also tired of losing cattle to every trail herd that comes through. Or having our cattle drift south in the winter. Now what about it? You want a job?"

I jerked my neck toward where the Tinhorn was still sitting. "We got another partner."

Ormsby sighted over my shoulder. He said, "Don't look like much."

"He's a gambler. By profession. Got anything he can do? He ain't much with a gun."

Ormsby shook his head. "No, we ain't hiring no professional gamblers. At least not right now."

"What about law?" I asked. "What are they going to think?"

"There is no law," he said. "There's one old sheriff in Tascosa and he knows this is none of his business."

I glanced at Wilcey and he shrugged. I tell you I almost wanted to laugh at myself. If somebody had told me even two days before that I'd be fixing to hire on for wages I'd have laughed in his face. But strange circumstances make for strange doings. I said, "We could use a little advance. We need to buy some new equipment and we'd like to have a good time for a day or two. We been on the trail a long time."

"Sure," Ormsby said. He reached in his pocket and peeled off a hundred dollars and handed it to me. "Split it between you. That enough?"

I nodded and stood up. "Yeah."

He pointed at the money in my hand. "We ain't giving that away."

Then I did almost laugh. "Oh, don't worry Mister Ormsby. We'll show up at your ranch headquarters. Ready to go to work. If we change our minds we'll get the money back to you before we spend it." I looked at Gaines. "We wouldn't want to put Mister Gaines here to any trouble coming to get it back."

Ormsby smiled slightly. "You catch on quick."

I give him a look. "It ain't that complicated, Ormsby. Don't kid yourself."

Then, just as we started away, Gaines spoke for the first time. Looking at me he said, "I know you."

"No you don't," I said quickly. "A lot of men look alike and many a mistake has been made about identity. Them kind of mistakes can get dangerous."

He made no sign and we turned and walked away. Passing the table I told the Tinhorn, "Bring the bottle and let's go to the hotel. We got some talking to do."

Chapter Two

We didn't say much until we got back to the hotel. Then Wilcey said, "Will, what the hell are we doing?"

There were two beds in the room. Wilcey and I had taken one each and the Tinhorn had taken all our bedrolls and made himself comfortable on the floor. We still had about three-quarters of the bottle of whiskey left and we had that sitting on the floor between us and we took an occasional pull out of it.

I said, "I'm damned if I know, Dennis." Then I started laughing.

Wilcey give me a look. "What the hell's so damned funny?" He had a kind of strained appearance on his face.

"I don't know," I said. "I just never had a job before. Never went up and actually *applied* for a job of wages before. Just strikes me as funny. Mister Ormsby trying to impress us with the size and holdings of that goddamn ranch. Hell, I'm near overcome, ain't you?"

"It ain't funny," he said. He lay back on his bed and stared up at the ceiling. Then he raised up again. "You sure we want to get into this?"

"Hell, we got to," I said, straight-faced. "We done took the money. And if we don't show up—why that Mister Gaines will come around wanting it back. And anybody can see he's a bad *hombre*."

The Tinhorn put in, "What the hell are ya'll talking about?"

"Take a drink of whiskey," I told him. "We'll lay it all out in a minute."

Wilcey said, "God damnit, Wilson, what was going on between you and that Gaines feller? You was both swelled up like a couple of Brahma bulls. Both had your necks bowed."

I shook my head, feeling serious. "It's just part of the game," I said. "He recognized me for what I am and I recognized him. Like a couple of buck elks waiting to butt heads."

"Is it going to be trouble?"

I looked up at him. I'd never expected to hear such a question from him. "What?" I asked him.

"Is there going to be trouble between you and him?"

"What the hell difference does it make?" I asked him, a touch of anger in my voice. "What the hell you worrying about a pearl-handle lackey like him for? You figure I can't handle *him*?"

He didn't say anything and I suddenly leaned back on the bed I was sitting on and looked at my two partners, looking at myself also. My God, I thought, we've gotten timid.

It was the only word I could think of to cover the way we were acting. I'd seen broncs brought in from the range, wild, tough, making their own way, having gotten a living for themselves off the ground, and then some bronc twister had gotten hold of them and next thing you'd see them standing in a corral, off in a corner, their head down, trembling, waiting for their bait of grain. Well, it didn't seem so much different for the three of us. But I, by God, wasn't going to stand for it. I sat up and looked at my partners. "I've had about enough of this shit," I said evenly. "We've been on a bad run of luck, but that don't mean it's going to go on forever. And by God I'm getting tired of seeing you two being down with your head under you. Now we're in a little bit of a tight, but that don't mean it's going to go on that way. I don't like doing this any better than you do. But we'll do it for the time being because we have to and we'll do it until we figure out something better. It'll give us a little stake and it'll give us a reason for being here so nobody won't get too curious."

Wilcey looked down at the floor and didn't say anything. Tinhorn said, "I wish to hell I knew what was going on."

"Tell him," I told Wilcey.

Wilcey laid it out for him. When he was through, the Tinhorn said, "What the hell am I supposed to do?"

"We're going to stake you to a hundred. You're going to stay in Tascosa and gamble."

"A hundred? That ain't much."

"Stay out of the big games. You're going to be playing cowboys that make forty a month. If you can't beat them you ought not to call yourself a professional gambler."

"How come they don't want me for that fence job?"

"Because you'd get yore ass killed, that's why."

"I been doing all right."

"Listen," I said, "will you get it through your head: you ain't no gunhand!"

He said, a little stiffly, "I been holding up my end."

"Oh, shit," I said in disgust. There ain't nothing much more dangerous to himself than somebody like the Tinhorn who's gotten a little taste of gunplay and thinks he's an expert. "Wilcey," I said, "tell him."

Wilcey said, "You better listen to Will. You ain't no gunhand. The few jobs you been in on, it was Will making the play. Wasn't nobody paying any attention to you or I. They was occupied with Will. But you get off in a storm by yourself and you're going to get some daylight let through you."

"Well . . ." he said.

"It won't be all that long," I told him. "Just until I can figure something out."

We went to bed not long after, then got up the next morning and spent the day just lounging around, letting our horses rest, resting ourselves, eating pretty good, drinking a little whiskey. Wasn't any need to try and save money now. Where Wilcey and I were going we wouldn't need any. We didn't see either Ormsby or Gaines the balance of the time we were out on the town.

I had trouble getting to sleep that night. We'd seen a few dance-hall girls in some of the saloons we'd been in and, ugly and low-class as they were, they'd been enough to set my mind pouring back over the trail of women I'd known and all the trouble they'd been. Of course the first one, the main one, had always been that high-born Spanish girl that I'd met on her uncle's hacienda after Tod had drowned his horse and lost us the $4,000 when we were trying to cross a flood-swole Rio Grande. She'd been the one I'd pursued for well over two years. She'd been the one that had caused me to vow that the job on the Uvalde bank would be my last one. That after that I was going to have enough money to buy respectability. It had been her I was pursuing down in Sabinas Hidalgo when I'd got the telegram about Les lying near to death in Nuevo Laredo. And it had been her that I'd robbed the train for. The train that Chulo the black Mexican and Chauncey Jones and I had taken $30,000 out of. The $30,000 I was going to use my part of to go, again, to Sabinas and buy me a horse ranch and woo her and convince her family I was quality and marry her and set up for respectability and peace. Only to get to Sabinas and discover she'd been married six months before.

But the worst mistake I'd made in that affair had

been abandoning a good woman to chase a dream. That had been Chulo's cousin's sister. A good woman, a comely woman, a woman who loved me and only wanted to please me. I was with her several months in San Antonio—Cata was her name—while we were planning the train robbery. And why I'd been so blind to her virtues was more than I could understand about myself. But I'd passed her by and, as soon as I'd had the train's gold in my hands, I'd been off again to chase my dream. Sometimes I wondered what might have happened if I'd succeeded in my quest. Probably she would have turned out to be a spoiled, ill-tempered, selfish woman who was too beautiful for her own good and too used to having every man she met kill himself to please her.

I sometimes thought of Cata. I sometimes wondered what she was doing. After the high-born Mexican girl had been put forever out of my reach, I'd briefly considered going back for Cata, but I was too ashamed of myself to do so. And, also, I'd treated her very badly and she probably wouldn't have wanted me back.

And I wondered how old Chulo was doing. He'd lost an eye in the train robbery, which must have made him a sight. Before that he'd been one of the meanest-looking sonofabitches you could imagine, but that closed eye could only add to the devilness of his face. I half smiled, remembering how he'd slit the nostril of the railroad clerk to make him tell us where the gold was and how the clerk had almost fainted just looking at Chulo.

Oh, he was a mean one all right, but a hell of a good man to have by your side on a rough job.

Then had come that other damn Linda, that half-Irish, half-Mexican woman I'd met in Juarez and who I'd lived with while we were planning the poker-game robbery. Oh, she was going to be the one. I was going to take her to California with me. Might even have married her. Almost felt like I loved her, if I'd ever really known what that meant outside of dreams and the unreachable. She'd been helping us on the robbery, acting as a drink waitress for the poker game so we'd know the layout when we went in to pull it. I'd even given her a thousand dollars. And she'd been supposed to be waiting for me at the hotel after the robbery and I was going to take her with us. The only thing was she hadn't been waiting. All that had been waiting had been a note saying she couldn't take my kind of life.

She'd run out on me as had so many before.

Run off with a goddamn shyster lawyer and two-bit politician that walked around in a goddamn suit with a vest on underneath. I'd always figured, all my life, to never trust one of them sonofabitches that had to have three pieces to his suit. Them goddamn careful little nit-picking three-piece-suit sonofabitches that didn't have enough balls to face a man, but had to beat him by slipping around and back-stabbing and stealing a man's woman with carefulness.

Oh, I loved them kind. Only thing I hated about it was I hadn't killed enough of them. You give me an honest goddamn outlaw every time.

And what did she mean about she couldn't take my kind of life? What the hell did she know about what kind of life I wanted? She hadn't known a goddamn thing but she'd thought she did. So she'd jumped to her own goddamn conclusion and run out on me for a goddamn paper shuffler. Well, I hoped she and him would come to no more bad of an end than being gut shot.

I reckoned there was a great deal of misconception out about me. I reckon all folks saw me as a killer and outlaw, a man just naturally made to have a revolver in his hand. I reckon they thought that's what I wanted. Well, they'd probably have a hard time believing that this outlaw wanted a wife and a home and a settled life. I'd see other men with that and I'd think, hell, they ain't any smarter or more capable than I am, and yet they have the very thing I want. I don't know; it just seemed somehow that I wasn't fated for that. But that didn't mean I was going to give up trying to get it. I'd get it somehow, someday. Some way there was, out there, what I was looking for. I went to sleep on that.

We rode out next morning heading for Tascosa. It was still blue-cold, but now the horses were rested and fed and we were feeling somewhat better ourselves. We made the forty-mile ride by mid-afternoon, and came cantering into the little town in pretty good style. It was pretty much like most other Panhandle towns I'd seen, weather-beaten, wind-blown, and sandblasted. Maybe it had a few more saloons than usual, but it had about the same number of houses and stores, and the one hotel that didn't do all that much business. Wilcey and I still had another five miles to go to the Skillet Ranch headquarters so we just took time to have one drink with the Tinhorn at a saloon. We wanted to make the ranch before dark, not wanting to get caught out in that cold after the sun went down.

The Tinhorn was going to hole up in the hotel. But he said, "What am I going to do if my money runs out?"

I looked over in the corner where a two-bit game was going on between five cowboys. "Like I told you," I said, "if you can't beat this bunch of ranch hands you ought not to call yourself a gambler. If you ain't got more money a month from now when we get back into town, I'm going to be severely disappointed in you."

We got away not too long after that, leaving the Tinhorn all the money we had. We left him with about a hundred and twenty dollars, having spent the balance on ten bottles of whiskey, which was going to be little enough considering the state of the weather.

Once out of town we put the horses in an easy lope, which they were willing to do, what with the rest they'd had.

I told Wilcey, "I feel like a schoolboy trying to figure out some way to play hooky."

"I know what you mean," he said. "I ain't exactly looking forward to this myself."

We rose the ranch out of the prairie not too much after, and went cantering in through the big storegate. The headquarters was about a mile on farther. The ranch was damn near as big as Tascosa. They had a power of buildings there, mostly sheds and barns and what I took to be bunkhouses, but there was also one big house that pretty well had to be the headquarters. We got up to a bunch of corrals and noticed a couple of cowhands working around there, so we pulled up and asked where we could find Ormsby. One of them shook his head. "Ain't here." They were both staring at us curiously. "You be fence riders?"

I nodded. One of them, tall, gaunt, and bewhiskered, pointed toward the main house. "Reckon you'll find Bob Danning in there in his little office. He kind of swamps for Ormsby."

We thanked them and cantered on up to the back of the big house, tying our horses at a hitching post. "Pretty swell-looking joint, ain't it?" I told Wilcey. We clumped up some little stairs and onto a big porch and stopped in front of a door. "We supposed to knock?"

"Hell if I know," Wilcey said.

I went ahead and knocked and, in a moment, the door was opened by a fellow that looked about half clerk, half foreman. He was a short, stocky man with enough gray in his hair to be about fifty. He was wearing good quality ranch clothes, but he had a pair of spectacles on his nose and was wearing a set of them cuffs that clerks wear when they're doing their book work.

"Yeah?" he said.

"We're looking for a man named Danning."

"I'm him. What do you want?"

I said, "Ormsby hired us for your fence. My name's Wilson. His is Dennis."

"Oh, yeah," he said. He stepped back in the room. "Come on in." He sat down behind a desk that had papers and ledgers spread all over it. We sat down in a couple of chairs across from him. There was a little fire burning in a fireplace to our side, but it was enough since the office wasn't all that big.

"Wilson and Dennis, huh," he said. He picked up a big ledger and wrote something in it, our names I guessed. Then he said, "Ormsby told you about the job?"

I nodded.

"Then you know what's expected?"

"Just don't let nobody mess with the fence."

"That's about it." He nodded. "With any means you have to use. If you run into more than you can handle, one of you goes for help."

"We understand," I said.

He got up from behind his desk and walked up to a map on the side wall. "I'm going to put you . . ." He studied the map a minute and then took out a pencil and drew a circle around some mark on the map. "Put you here, at the second camp. That's thirty miles east of here. You understand you're responsible for fence five miles west of your camp and ten miles east."

We just nodded and he came back to his desk. He said, "It's coming on late so ya'll find yoreselfs a place in one of the bunk houses, then hunt up our headquarters foreman, Joe Sawyer, at supper and he'll see about getting you outfitted and grubbed and lettin' you pick yore remuda. That's about all. Get that done early enough in the mornin' to make your camp before dark tomorrow night."

We got up. I almost felt like touchin' my hat brim to him, but I didn't. Which shows you how low I'd come.

We located the bunkhouse, found us a couple of bunks that didn't have any bed clothes on 'em and slung our bedrolls and saddles down. Our horses were still tied outside, but I figured somebody would tell us what to do with them. The bunkhouse was deserted, it still being working hours, so Wilcey and I just sat down and lit cigarillos and didn't say anything. Finally I heaved myself up. "Hell," I said to Wilcey, "I'm dry as all get out. Think I'll step out to the saddlebags and have a pull."

"Myself," Wilcey said. He got up and followed me out the door and over to the horses. I took a bottle of whiskey out and handed it to Wilcey. He had a pull and then handed it to me. I was about to up with it myself when I felt a touch on my shoulder. I looked around and there was this kidlike-looking cowhand. He said, "I wouldn't be doing that."

Now, he wasn't actually any kid, but he was kind of fat-looking and didn't appear to have much brains in his face. I said, "Wouldn't be doing what?"

"It's against company regulations to be drinking intoxicating beverages on company land."

I was so astounded I didn't know what to say. He sounded like some kid who'd gotten his lessons up at home and was recitin' 'em next day in school. He was even breaking up some of the long words so that they sounded like two or three strung together. I'd taken the bottle down from my lips and looked at Wilcey. He just shrugged and looked about half ready to laugh. Then I looked around at this here jayhoo and said, "Say what?"

And be damned if he didn't set out to quote me what he'd got up by heart again. But I broke in on him. "No, no," I said. "Hold up. You trying to tell me I ain't supposed to drink on this ranch?"

"That's it, Mister," he said. "Them's company regulations."

I looked over at Wilcey and he was examining the hired hand like he was looking at some strange kind of bug.

"I be go to hell," I said, marveling.

And this jack rabbit said, "Understand I'm telling you for your own good. You may be passing through or you may be a new hired hand, but if Mister Sawyer ketches you you'll be on your way anyhow. Mister Sawyer don't hold with breaking company rules."

I reckoned *Mister* Sawyer to be the foreman we were supposed to do business with. I turned around and took a good look at this Skillet cowboy. Then I upped with the bottle and had a pull. Then I handed it to Wilcey. "Run along, boy," I said.

"I'm just telling you what—"

"Run along, I said!" I was getting slightly put out. "It's cold out here and I don't want to stand around talking with the likes of you."

"All right, but I was—"

"I said, GIT!"

Well, he took off then and I finally reckoned it was funny. At least me and Wilcey started laughing. "Hell," I said, "now that we know the rules, let's take the bottle back in the bunkhouse so we can drink out of the cold."

"Might as well."

We went back in the bunkhouse, still laughing. I didn't know whether we were laughing because it was funny or because we'd got ourselves into such a fix that we should be subjected to such embarrassment as

WILSON'S CHOICE 35

to be told what we could do by some roly-poly snot-nosed hired hand.

But then, we were hired hands too.

But we did sit down on our bunks with the bottle between us and commenced to have a few drinks.

We were doing that when a few of the cowhands began to drift in. We were toward the back of the building and I was sitting on the bunk facing the door so I could see them as they come wandering in. They glanced our way, but none of them gave us a howdy or offered to come over and speak.

Which was all right with us, except it didn't quite seem in keeping with the custom of the country.

But I was already getting the feeling that the Skillet Ranch didn't exactly run to the custom of the country.

A little louder than was necessary I asked Wilcey, "Wonder who the owners of this ranch are? Yankees?"

For whom I had no love, as you can understand. Not after what happened to my family after the Civil War.

And Wilcey said, also in a kind of loud voice, "From Chicago, I believe."

A few of the cowhands up at the other end of the bunkhouse glanced our way, but they didn't say anything. Me and Wilcey had another drink.

"Ain't too friendly around here, is it?" I asked him, still in that loud voice.

"That's Yankees for you," he said.

But we still didn't get any rise. "Hell with it," I said. "We're acting a little foolish. Reckon we better pull our horns in until we get the lay of the land a little better."

Well, we sat there, smoking and drinking, being given a good letting alone. But, not too much later, this big raw-boned-looking hand come in. He stopped inside the door, looking around. Then he spotted us and come straight back, his spurs jingling on the hard floor. It was still plenty cold in the bunkhouse even though one of them hands had gotten a pot-bellied stove going. This jayhoo pulled up in front of us. He looked to be about forty years of age and looked like a man used to giving orders. He give us a look, his eyes taking in the bottle and our general attitude, which wasn't too respectful. He said, "You be Dennis and Wilson?"

"That's about it," I said. "And you'd be *Mister* Sawyer."

I was kind of lounged back on the bunk looking up at him. His face, which wasn't any too pretty, kind of swelled up and got red around the veins in his nose.

He said, in a voice that was a little too tight, "You two are fence riders. And I'm supposed to git you ready to pull out tomorrow. But you get that bottle of whiskey outen this bunkhouse or I'll break it and you both. I ain't afeered of you gunnies!"

Well, from the way he was talking I figured he already had his orders about me and Wilcey. So I said, "Listen, Sawyer, just do your job. Don't give us none of your shit."

"Why—" he said, and started to reach for my arm. But I outed with my revolver and shoved it in his belly. His face got a surprised look. He froze.

"Listen, Sawyer," I said, "take it easy or I'm going to make your back look like your front. Namely, they'll be a hole in both of them. Now, you take yore tent revival and pass on out of here and don't bother us no more. You understand?"

He gawked, but he didn't move. Across the opposite bunk Wilcey was laughing quietly. I guess we'd both come to the place where we'd had just about enough. I said, "You understand me?"

He didn't speak, just began to back away. Ten feet toward the door he said, "I'll have you both fired."

"Do us that favor," I said.

He turned and went on out without another word. I turned to Wilcey and said, "I ought not to have done that."

Which made him start laughing. "No," he said, "you really ought not to have." But the end of his sentence was drowned out with his laughing.

"No, I mean it," I said.

Which made him laugh even harder. "Yeah, I know you do."

"Well, the hell with you." But I was laughing so hard myself I couldn't get any force in it.

I knew we were both about half drunk and about enough disgusted with the sorry end we'd come to that neither one of us cared if school kept, but I also knew that that old dog wouldn't hunt for long. If we got thrown out on our ear we'd be in an even worse plight—out in the cold and broke and with nowhere to go. We were going to have to pull our horns in and quit playing the fool.

But I couldn't stop laughing. I sat up and swung around and told Wilcey, "Now, listen, you got to get hold of yourself. The boss has done told us to get rid of this whiskey and all you're doing is laying on your bunk laughing your goddamn head off." I reached down, got the bottle and had a pull. "Well, listen, that won't get it. Now, I can't get rid of this whiskey all by myself so you are going to have to pull yourself together and give me a little help."

He didn't move so I had another pull. "God damnit, Wilcey," I said, "I'm warning you."

"All right," he finally said. He swung his legs around and sat up and took the bottle from me. "But I'm telling you, this stuff ain't good for a body, and you oughtn't to be makin' me drink it."

"I know," I said. "But *Mister* Sawyer done told us to get rid of it. What am I supposed to do?"

Well, we sat there slugging down the rest of that

bottle of whiskey, getting a little drunker all the time. Part of the problem was that we hadn't eaten a bit of food all day. I looked over Wilcey's shoulder toward the other end of the bunkhouse. They was six or seven of them hands gathered up down there. They were giving a big appearance of not paying any attention to us, but I could see first one and then the other cutting their eyes our way every once in a while. Finally I raised up and yelled at them. "Hey! Hey!"

Not a one of them looked around. "Hey, god damn-it! I'm talking to you!"

They still acted like we were at the North Pole or somewheres. Which, it being about as cold as it was, I could understand. But I yelled, "When in the goddamn hell is supper?"

Finally a tall young yahoo, wearing his longjohns and hat, kind of turned our way. He said, "What was that, mister?"

"I said when in the goddamn hell is supper?"

"Pretty quick now."

"Where's it at?"

"Well, just out yonder. Ya'll follow us and we'll show you."

I said, "Come here, boy."

He didn't much want to, but he finally did. He come up kind of nervous and not too sure what he was doing there. I didn't help him much when I asked him if he knew how silly he looked wearing his underwear and his hat. I said, "Either take the goddamn hat off or put on your clothes."

He said, "Yes, sir," and took off his hat.

I looked at Wilcey. "My God, look at this boy. He thinks he's at the ball." Then I turned back to him. "Put your hat on, boy. We ain't gov'ment officials."

"Yes, sir," he said.

"And don't call me sir. I ain't your goddamn boss. What's your name?"

"Tom," he said.

I was getting a little ashamed of myself. I said, "Well, Tom, tell you the truth, we ain't as bad as we look. We're just both off our range and a little drunk. You whistle us up when it comes time to eat and I'll be much obliged."

"Yes, sir," he said.

"Put your hat back on, boy. We ain't shot nobody all day and if we don't shoot somebody by six of an afternoon we give up on it. And it's way past that time now. Now, you go on back to your bunkmates."

"Yes, sir," he said.

When he was gone I looked at Wilcey. "Ever get the feeling you been talking to a fence post?"

"Yes, sir," was all he said.

"It ain't that long past six," I said.

Well, Tom did whistle us up and we went over and ate in the grub-house. I was amazed at the number of cowhands that were in the place. They were two long tables and I figured there were at least sixty people being served, with about ten others waiting table. We had a good meal of steak and potatoes and some kind of poke salad greens and plenty of sour-dough bread and gravy. I told Wilcey that I could fault the people that ran the ranch for a lot of things, but not for the feed. Sawyer was in there and he saw us and we saw him, but he never said a word or even much looked in our direction. We were sitting on benches shoved up to the table and passing the various dishes down to our left and right and the only time we caught eyes was just briefly when I was handing down a platter of beefsteak to the man beside him.

Other than that there was nothing.

But then, as Wilcey and I were walking back to the bunkhouse, this boy Tom passed us and said, "Ya'll watch out. Mister Sawyer is layin' for ya'll."

Which surprised the shit out of me. I'd figured him for a man who wouldn't hold a grudge.

I said to Wilcey, "What you reckon we ought to do? Saddle up and leave tonight?"

He said, "Aw, hell. Let's hope we get lucky and he won't hurt us over much."

We went to bed on that. I told Wilcey, "Don't tremble in your sleep. It'll be a dead giveaway."

I had taught Wilcey a little trick Les and I used to use. If you've got two men sleeping in the same room and you want one of them, you can come in and put a gun on him and get his revolver out from under his pillow or off the bedside table or off the bedstead, wherever he's got it, and you can do this without waking his partner. But you can't do that if he and his partner take a piece of string and tie it to each other's thumb. Because they ain't going to think to disarm the partner, most times, and then all you've got to do, when they're waking you up with a gun in your face and think they got you, is to twitch that string and, all of a sudden, they got your partner with his gun in their back.

And most folks find that a very uncomfortable way to live.

Which is about what happened. I reckon that Sawyer had figured I was the more dangerous one of the pair because they woke me sometime later that night. It was him and another man. They had a gun in my face and a hand over my mouth when I came awake. Sawyer was saying, "All right, gunnie. You just keep your mouth shut. We going to get you off this here ranch where honest folk live. Now, get up!"

Well, naturally, I raised up just as nice as pie, not wanting to give anybody any trouble. I said, "Yes, sir. Whatever you say." But at the same time I gave my string thumb a pretty good twitch. They never took any notice. Sawyer said, "Now, git yore cornbread ass outen that bed."

"God damnit, Sawyer," I said, trying to keep their attention on me, "it's cold as hell. I don't want to get out of this warm bed."

"God damnit!" he said. "You mind when yore told to." And be damned if he didn't slap me across the face. I never flinched. He wasn't holding a gun on me, but the man he was with was and I didn't know how quick he'd be to shoot.

About that time Wilcey said, from behind them, "Hello."

They froze. Then Sawyer took a quick look back, only to see Wilcey sitting on the side of his bunk holding a revolver very steadily on them.

"We got company," I said.

Sawyer said to Wilcey, "You better be careful. We got a gun on yore partner."

"He knows that," I said.

Sawyer said, "Then he knows he better put that pistol away or we're going to blow a hole clean through you."

"No," I said, "you got it wrong. In the first place, I don't think either you or this other yahoo ever shot a man. Dennis has. Plenty of times. And he likes it. What's going to happen is he's going to shoot both of you in the back in about the next five seconds if you don't get that gun out of my face and get the hell out of here."

Sawyer, not sounding very certain, said, "First man gets shot is going to be you."

"Maybe," I said. "I been shot before and I'm still here to talk about it. But I can guarantee you one thing. You may shoot me and you may kill me, but Dennis will for sure kill both of you."

The man with Sawyer said, "Listen, maybe we better get out of here. I didn't bargain for none of this." He uncocked the pistol he was holding and sort of took a small step backward. When he did I reached up and jerked the revolver out of his hand, reversed it, cocked it, and stuck it between Sawyer's eyes.

"Now, listen, pigshit," I said, "get your goddamn hands up and make it snappy! Now!"

He had my revolver stuck down in his belt and I jerked that out and dropped it on the bed beside me. Then I commenced easing out of the bed.

Wilcey said, "What you going to do, Will?"

"Not much," I said. I suddenly hit Sawyer a full-swinging backhanded slap. "Don't ever touch me again, or I'll kill you. You understand?" He didn't say anything so I slapped him again. "I asked you if you understood I'd kill you if you ever messed with me again. Do you understand me?"

Down the way in the bunkhouse I could see men raising up in their beds, awakened by the commotion. I gave Sawyer another full-handed slap just for them.

"Do you understand?" I asked him again. I tapped the barrel of the revolver against his teeth. "You better tell me something, shit-eater, before I kill you now. Do you understand not to mess with me again?"

"Yes," he finally said. But it was weak and unsteady.

"No! Loud! Let me hear you, piss-head, or I'll shoot your balls off, if you got any!"

"Yes," he said.

"Louder!"

"Yes!"

"Louder!"

"YES!"

I slapped him once more just so he wouldn't forget and then told him, "Now, you two goat-suckers get your asses out of here and don't come back."

The other man said, "What about my pistol?"

"It'll be laying on this bed in the morning. I wouldn't come for it before then. Now get!"

They left and Wilcey and I sat down and got out a couple of cigarillos and lit them. "Thanks," I said to him.

"Hell of a way to wake up," he said.

"Yeah. Hell of a way to get started on whatever we call what it is we're doing."

"How bad you reckon we're fucked up?"

I shrugged. "Damned if I know. I'm brand-new at this job business."

"Reckon they'll run us off?"

I yawned. I was getting sleepy again. "I doubt it. I kind of get the feeling the fence riders are a little different from their day-to-day hired hands. I reckon they'll put up with a little bullshit from us." I put my cigarillo out on the floor. "But the hell with it. Let's get some sleep."

Next morning, right after breakfast, a short, chunky hand came up to us. "My name is Upton," he said. "I'm the ramrod here at the headquarters ranch." He had a kind of little twinkle in his eye. "For some reason Mister Sawyer don't feel up to gettin' ya'll outfitted so I reckon I've drawed that chore. Ya'll about ready?"

I said that I reckoned we were and he took us around and we drawed our supplies and picked out our remuda. I said, "We're taking our own saddle horses with us."

He kind of shrugged. "You can do that, but you ain't supposed to feed them company grain."

"Oh, we wouldn't think of it," I said. "Would we, Wilcey?"

"No, indeed. No, indeed."

We got all lined out, but before we could get away, Ormsby and Gaines showed up. We were out near the bunkhouse tying our packs and other gear on a couple of the horses. Ormsby and Gaines came up and Ormsby said, "Listen, Wilson, I've heard about what happened with you two and I want you to know I don't like it one damn bit."

I went on with my work. I said, "Yeah, don't blame you. I didn't like it too much myself."

"Don't give me none of your smart talk," he said. "We've got regulations on this ranch and every man that draws wages here is going to abide by them."

He sounded angry. I hadn't turned around to see them. Wilcey was on the other side of the horse from me and I knew I could read in his face anything that was about to happen. I said, "First time I heard about your rules was when we got told in a very quarrelsome manner. I don't know about you, but I ain't much taken by people coming at me in a quarrelsome manner."

"By God," he said, "I'm about half a mind to run you both off."

I said, "Yeah, I've heard of men making that mistake."

He said sharply, "What mistake?"

"Doing something with only half their mind made up." I turned around. He was standing there with Gaines just behind him. The gunman was like always—his face set, not saying anything. He was chewing on a toothpick. I said, "Man decides to do something he ought to have his whole mind made up. Otherwise it might turn out kind of bad."

Ormsby stared at me a long second and then said, "You better be about half as good as you think you are." Then he turned around and walked off. Gaines give me one glance then followed him.

Wilcey said, "I don't believe them two old boys like you, Will."

"And I can't understand why."

We got away about mid-morning, riding east, following the fence line. It had warmed up to about twenty degrees, which seemed like we were back down in Mexico, cold as it had been the night before. We had about fifteen miles to go so we pressed it pretty good. I tell you I had never seen such barren country; just unbroken plains for miles and miles. The damn country even looked cold. Wilcey glanced up at the sky, which was low and gray. "It'll snow tonight if I ain't mistaken," he said.

"Probaby snow every night," I said.

We made a nooning, eating some cold meat and biscuits that the cook had given us and washing it down with coffee and whiskey.

"We better go slow on this whiskey," Wilcey cautioned. "We ain't got over much."

"Ain't that the truth," I agreed. "In fact we ain't got over much of nothin' except plains and cold and cowchips."

We made our line camp about mid-afternoon. To say that it wasn't much ain't quite catching the flavor of the place. It was a little raw lumber shanty with a sod roof and a fair-sized horse pen out in the back. They'd even used the drift fence for the back part of the horse lot.

"Well, here's home," I said. We got down, a little stiff from the long ride. "Might as well unload quick as we can and get a fire going."

While Wilcey carried our gear inside I led the horses around to the corral and turned them in and commenced unloading the grain we'd bought for them. We only had about four hundred pounds, which wouldn't last long, not with what little grass there was, but Upton had told us a supply wagon would be along in the next week with more water and more feed. I'd taken notice that there were only two barrels of water set out in the corral. I hoped there was another barrel inside for Wilcey and me. I shouldn't say barrels of water, but barrels of ice, for it was frozen pretty thick, even as early in the day as it was. Come night it would probably get solid.

I got the horses tended to and then went on inside. Soon as I was in the door I took a look around and said, "Well, I see they ain't plannin' on spoiling us none."

"Indeed not," Wilcey said. He was busy stacking our grub in the corner. We had potatoes and bacon and a sack of flour and coffee and a little sugar and some canned goods. We'd also been told we could kill a beeve if we needed to but to be sure and record the brand. There was also a barrel of water in the corner. I found a dipper and lifted the lid and had a drink. It was pretty brackish, but it was drinkable.

The main problem was going to be the cold. Whoever had built the cabin out of the raw lumber hadn't made too much effort about getting his joints close together. There were holes in every wall and the wind just came whistling through. All we had for heating, and I suppose for cooking, was a little cast-iron stove. It wasn't going to be much against those Panhandle blizzards. It was already so cold in the cabin that our water had ice in it.

I said to Wilcey, "Guess I better get in a load of cow-chips and get a fire going. If you can find some old rags, or even some of your old clothes, why don't you take them and try and stop up some of them holes in the walls?"

"Okay, but I'll use some of your clothes."

I found a tow-sack and went out on the bald-ass prairie and commenced gathering up a load of dried cow-chips. Of course that was all we had to burn as there hadn't been a tree in the country in about nine thousand years. But cow-chips do a good job if that's all you have. They put out a lot of heat. The only problem is they burn up fast and you've got to have a considerable supply to make do for a night.

Boy howdy, that wind was cutting right through me. And that was going to be another problem. Neither Wilcey nor I had any clothes that were really suitable for the country. I had a pretty good fleece-lined jacket, but it wasn't nearly thick enough, nor long enough, to shut out much of the cold.

I got my load and went on back in and, using some old paper, got a fire started in the stove. It caught on fast enough, but it wouldn't draw properly and nearly went out before I got the damper adjusted just so.

"Goddamn stove," I told Wilcey, "is as temperamental as a woman."

He'd found a couple more old feed-sacks and was trying to chink up the walls. I left him to it and began making a couple more trips after cow-chips. When I had enough to make the night and cook breakfast by, I knocked off and got the fire stocked up as big as I could. Then I routed out our sleeping gear and pitched Wilcey's on one bunk and mine on the other. The bunks weren't much—just wooden frames set against the walls with rawhide strapping for springs. There were no windows in the cabin and, as it was coming dark outside, I got a kerosene lantern lit and hung it to one of the rafters. It commenced to throw dancing shadows in the corners.

Wilcey said, "There. That's the best I can do. Besides, I'm out of tow-sacks."

He had managed to knock off some of the wind, but there was still a considerable amount whistling through.

"Hell with it," I said. "Let's have a drink of whiskey and worry about the election."

"What election?"

"Any of them. They're all the same."

I got out a bottle of whiskey while Wilcey dipped

up two tin cups about half full of cold water. We hit it pretty good with the whiskey, then took a seat on our bunks, facing each other, and toasted to luck.

"Luck."

"Luck."

Then we knocked them back. Sweetened up with the whiskey the cold water didn't taste half bad. Now that it was coming dark the wind was whistling even harder, but our little stove was putting out enough heat to, as Wilcey said, "keep the icicles off our ears."

We had supper to fix and then the problem of how we were going to sleep in the damn icebox we were in but, for the time being, it was comfortable just to sit and let the whiskey take a little of the chill out of our bones. We didn't say much while we drank that first drink. When I got up to mix us another, Wilcey threw some coffee and water in the pot and set it on the stove to get us some coffee going. Then we sat back down. Now that it was dark the lantern couldn't do much more than light the center of the room. All the corners were dark.

"I damn well hope we got enough bedding," I said.

"We drawed four extra blankets at the ranch. What with what we already had that ought to make do."

We sat there drinking our second drink. Wilcey asked me, "Will, is this about the worst fix you ever found yourself in?"

I thought about that a minute. "Well, they's been plenty of times I been in more eminent danger of being kilt. And I been broke before and when you're broke you are out of money, which is about as broke as you can get. And I been just as bad on the run, just as bad wanted." I thought some more. "I don't know, Wilcey. When I was a young man and first taking to the owl-hoot trail it didn't seem so bad because I kind of thought of it as a passing fancy. Something I'd do until I extricated myself and went on to a decent life.

Just never thought it would go on and on, if you understand what I mean. Now I feel like my sand is running out and that I'm branded as what I am and it'll never change. That kind of takes hope away from me and sort of makes everything just a little bit harder. It's like I ain't got nothing to look forward to, nothing to say about, 'Well, when I get out of this bad spot things will turn for the better and I'll be all right.' Only now I'm beginning to believe that if I get out of this bad spot, they'll just be another one waiting for me. This place bothers me some more than most because I feel like I've let a little of my pride slip away. This business with Ormsby and Sawyer. I know we done all right with that, but I still don't like being in the position where a man can approach me like them two did. And I goddamn sure don't like being here. But what I think I don't like the most is that we ain't got no prospects. Hell, I can't even think of a goddamn thing to rob! And that's getting in a pretty low bind. I mean, who the hell we going to hold up out here that's got any kale at all? Cows? Nestors?" I took a drink of my whiskey. Wilcey was watching me. "Yeah," I said, "I guess maybe. I guess maybe it is now that I think of it. And I reckon it's the lack of any prospects that makes it so goddamn bad. Look at us! Stuck out here in a blizzard with nothing but a shithouse shanty to keep the cold off. Hell, that's a pretty sorry comedown."

The coffee boiled over and Wilcey got up to fetch it. Using his hat for a hot-pad, he picked up the big pot, came over and poured me some in my cup and then did the same for his own. I held the warm tin cup between my palms, letting it take the chill out of my hands.

"Any of what I've said make any sense?"

He looked away. "Yeah. Unfortunately it does. I guess the reason I asked the question is I'm feeling about the same." He walked over and spit on the stove, making it sizzle.

I could hear the low tone in his voice and I had half an idea what was bothering him. "It gettin' under your saddle blanket, coming back to this country again?"

"Damn right it is," he said. "What'd you think?"

I let that slide. Hoping to change the subject I asked, "Well, is this about the worst ever come to you? Or, what was the worst?"

"Oh, I don't know," he said. "I guess after the old lady run out and taken the kids and I stayed drunk and lost the ranch. About the time I found myself laying behind a livery stable in Sweetwater, Texas, with a cold wind blowing, and I knew I didn't have the price of a drink, much less a meal or a room. I guess I was out of options about then, myself."

"What'd you do?" I asked him.

"Sold my saddle."

I whistled lightly. A man don't sell his saddle unless he's finally down to the bottom. "I bet that was hard," I said.

He looked up at me. "Why? I didn't have no horse to put it on. I'd sold that a week before."

I sort of half laughed. "Then what'd you do with the money you got for your saddle?"

"Stayed drunk. Tried to gamble. Ended up right where I'd been. Behind that livery stable without a cent."

These were things he'd never told me before. "So what'd you do then?"

He dropped his head. "That, I ain't going to tell you."

"Com'on, Wilcey. Don't come that on me."

"Nope. I ain't too proud of what I did."

"What? Rob your grandmother? Borrow offen an enemy?" I laughed.

He said, "No, I rolled a drunk in an alley."

Well, he looked so downright ashamed when he said it that I had to laugh again. "Oh, hell, Wilcey," I said, "if that's so bad you can't talk about it, then I'm in the same fix myself because I done it once also. Done it in Nuevo Laredo when I was so froze for a few dollars to have a drink and a good time on I didn't know what to do. I once had a pair of silver spurs I thought was the cat's whiskers. Well, I sold them, then got a little money ahead in a poker game and, when the old boy I'd sold them to wouldn't sell them back, I laid for him and bushwhacked him just as pretty as you please."

He shook his head. "Don't sound like the same thing to me."

"Oh, hogwash," I said. "I've done everything mean and lowdown there is to do except keep school. Don't come the dying calf on me." I drained my cup. "Now, let's fix some supper before we freeze to death."

We cooked up a batch of pancakes out of the flour we had and fried some bacon and with that and the coffee we made out pretty well. Before we left the stove Wilcey put on some potatoes to boil so we could fry them up next morning in the bacon grease we'd left standing in the skillet.

"My wife taught me to do that," he said. "Or at least she showed me what to do."

I said, a little hardness in my voice, "You remember in El Paso what a fool you told me I was making over that girl? Well, you're making a fool about your memories right now."

He didn't say anything, just glanced my way. Not too long after that we both went to bed. I was considerably tired and still a little cold so it felt good to crawl in under the heavy blankets and get some sleep. We'd stocked up the stove as full as we could, but I knew it'd be cold as a banker's heart by morning.

Chapter Three

We settled down to a way of life that I didn't much give a damn about. Early on Wilcey had warned, "Will, I got the feeling you are thinking we shouldn't ought to work at this job, just lay around until we ready to take off. Well, that won't work. They'll be checking on us and if they find out we're not checking that fence they'll tie a tin can to our tails. We going to have to do it if we want to stay here."

Well, he couldn't have been much righter, for that was exactly what I'd been thinking. But once he explained it to me I saw the light, so I resolved to bite the bullet and get on about the work of the Skillet Ranch, if for no other reason than we had no other choice.

We fell into a routine that divided up the work the best way we knew how. We had fifteen miles of fence, but the line camp wasn't positioned in the middle. To the west it was five miles to where the next rider was coming up from the other camp. But it was ten miles to the east and the boundary with the next camp's area of responsibility. One day Wilcey would take the five-mile patrol and I the ten and then we'd switch off the next day. Way we worked it was the man who had the five-mile run was responsible for housekeeping chores and seeing to the stock and getting in cow-chips and having supper ready and what not. The man that had the ten-mile patrol took off at daylight, with his noon meal packed, and got back in that night as early as he could. Neither one of the deals was exactly what I'd have called fun.

Evenings we ate supper, drank a little whiskey, played a few hands of seven-up on jawbone stakes, which meant payday stakes, then turned in, went to sleep, and started the whole thing over the next day.

After about a week of that I got in from the long run, about half-frozen, and told Wilcey, "You remember that goddamn Tinhorn when we left him? Left him with a hundred dollar stake in a town with saloons and houses and probably even a whore or two. You remember that?"

Wilcey said, yes, he remembered it.

"And you remember that sonofabitch standing there looking like he was losing his best friends?"

"Yes."

"Well, I got an idee. Why don't I go in and stand there looking like I'd lost my best friends and let him come out here and take my place. How's that?"

"No. I got a better idee. *I'll* go in and you and him ride these goddamn fences."

The hell of it was I felt like we was guardin' a piece of the North Pole that nobody in his goddamn right mind would want any part of, much less be ready to fight over. I knew, for my part, I would have been glad on one of those long rides to have seen an armed party come up and declare they were fixing to pull the fucking fence down. I wouldn't have given a goddamn about the fence but I would have been elated to have had a little diversion from the goddamn boredom and snow. At least it would have been a fight, a party of some kind, and that would have been better than looking at that endless, unchanging landscape.

It had began to snow. Not snow that banked up and buried you. The wind blew too hard for that, but flurries that swarmed around you and your horse and made it difficult to see even the very fence you were riding beside.

And then the very worst happened: we ran out of whiskey. We'd known it was coming even though we'd been conserving it as best we could. But after about two weeks, it had to happen. You've got to remember that, with two men cooped up by a fence line during the day, and by cabin walls during the night, even the best of pards can have a falling out. It's what they call cabin fever. It ain't either one of your fault, but it's going to happen just as sure as God made rain because man is man and that's just about the way of it. The one thing that had been the saving of us and the one thing that we'd looked forward to each night had been coming in from all that cold and snow and having a warming drink of coffee laced with whiskey. It would kind of settle us down from the bitterness we'd built up during our lonely day's trek. God knows, neight one of us was enjoying the life we were leading. We were trying to be considerate of the other's feelings, but we were, after all, just a couple of uncouth bandits, not Sunday-school teachers, and we didn't require much pushing. I came in one night from the ten-mile patrol, my blanket around my shoulders, and went up to the fire. Wilcey had gotten in earlier and he was sitting on his bunk with a cup of hot coffee between his hands sipping at it. I poured me out a cup and then looked around. "Where's the whiskey?" I asked him.

"Gone," he said.

I looked at him. "What you mean, gone?"

"I mean gone. We drank the last of it last night."

"Bullshit!" I said. "You mean you got the last of it in your cup."

He had irritation in his voice when he said, "Oh, come off it. This is straight coffee. You seen us drink the last of it last night. We talked about it. Don't come that shit on me."

"Then don't come it on me!" I said. I went over and sat down on my bunk. "You got whiskey in that cup. Look how you're cradling it between yore hands! Don't lie to me!"

"Oh, shit, Will," he said, sounding even more irritated. Which made me angry. "This ain't nothing but straight coffee. God damnit, you insisted on drinking up our last just last night. Don't tell me what I got in this cup! I'd by God like a drink of whiskey myself."

"You're lying!"

A little quiet fell over that cold shanty.

He said, "What's that you say?"

I said, "You're lying."

He looked down in his cup and didn't say anything for a moment. After a time he kind of sighed. "Well, you've put me in a fix."

"How's that?" I asked him. I was wearing my revolver and I kind of took it out and ran a finger down the barrel, like I was caressing it. He'd taken note.

"You didn't have to do that."

"Do what?"

"Out with that piece of iron."

I said, "I got a right to take my revolver out and examine it any time I want to. What are you, becoming an old maid?"

"Oh, shit, Will!" he said.

"And what's that supposed to mean?"

"Just this. Just what I said a minute ago about you putting me in a fix. You call me a liar. All right. I know I ain't no liar. But what's my options? I go up against you I get kilt. Ain't too many men can go up against you and win. Or else I sit here and let you call me a liar." His voice suddenly got steady. "Well, I don't happen to be no liar and I ain't going to sit here and let you call me one. Not if I get kilt for it." And he suddenly got up, stalked across to me, and threw his cup of coffee in my face.

With me sitting on my bunk holding my revolver in my hand.

I was so shocked, I didn't shoot him by instinct, praise God. And I mean that. For as the coffee trickled down my face I tasted it with my tongue and it was, as he'd said, straight coffee.

"Oh, shit!" I said. I slung my revolver over to the head of my bunk and kind of looked down. He was standing right over me, waiting to see what I'd do.

"Hell," I said.

"You sonofabitch," he called me.

"All right," I said. I kind of had my head down.

"Listen," he said, "I know I can't take you, but don't you come at me again, or I'll, by God, try."

He sounded so much like my old lost partner Les that I almost wept. I said, "All right."

He didn't wait for no further apology. I reckon he figured he'd already given about as much as I was capable of taking. Still with my head down I heard him walk back across the hard-packed floor. Then I heard them rawhide strapping springs sort of give as he sat down. When a little time had passed I looked up. I said, "Reckon we ought to try and get some supper?"

"Yeah," he finally said, "I reckon we ought to."

It had been a near thing, but that's the way it can happen when you are living under the kind of circumstances that Wilcey and I were under. Weren't neither one of us to blame, but it'll fall out like that some time.

Well, we got a little relief after that bad episode and I, for one, was not expecting it. I came riding in one evening, after the ten-mile patrol and, I tell you, I was tired and cold as hell. I was slumped in my saddle with a blanket wrapped around my shoulders. As I've said, the clothes Wilcey and I had were not fit for the country, so we'd taken to riding fence wrapped up like Indian braves. I had a bandanna tied over the top of my hat and under my chin, as much to keep my hat on as to keep my ears warm. Not a goddamn thing had happened, as usual, the whole fence ride. And I was coming back into our line camp wondering how much more of this I was going to take. Wilcey and I'd been staying the hell out of each other's range since we'd nearly gotten into it when the whiskey had run out. All we did now was to eat what supper there was, grunt at each other, and fall into bed.

No more card games. No more talk. Just acting like two old bears with a couple of sore paws.

I came in slowly, letting my pony, which was one of the Skillet remuda horses, stop to graze at the bunchgrass because I knew there'd be no hay for him in his horse corral.

I guess the only good thing I could say about that sorry-ass country was that the wind blowed so hard it blowed the snow off the ground, which allowed them sorry-ass cattle to be able to find the bunchgrass that allowed them to live.

It also blowed the snow off the ground so that we could find the cowshit in the form of cow-chips that allowed us to live.

Well, I finally found the line camp and rode up there and got off my horse, cold and stiff, and led him into the corral and unsaddled him, slinging my saddle into the corner where I knew it would be waiting for me next morning, and then, still hunched up in my blanket, went to the door and shoved it open.

It opened up on that flickeringly dim room that I knew so well. But, before I could step into the room, Wilcey was there, grabbing me by the shoulders.

"Hold it, Will," he said, "we got company."

I was carrying my Winchester by the barrel stock

and I immediately shifted it down so that my right hand was in contact with the trigger. But Wilcey started laughing. "Hold it! Hold it!" he said.

I said, "Oh, shit!" my mood being what it was, and jerked past him and took two steps into the room, my rifle up.

It was the Tinhorn, or the Preacher, as Wilcey called him, sitting on Wilcey's bunk, grinning like a coon eating catfish.

I stood a moment, tired and cold as I was, then I said, "Oh, shit," and kind of set my rifle down and set down on my bunk. "God damnit!" I said. "What are you doing here? I thought we was shut of you forever."

He said, "No chance."

Then Wilcey brought me over a cup of coffee. I took it, grateful for what little solace it might offer. But there was more solace in it than I'd figured—there was whiskey in it. I looked at him. "Thought you said we was out?"

He jerked his head toward the Tinhorn. "He brung it."

I took a deep drink, letting it go to my vitals, which were frozen. I said, "Well, it's about time the sonofabitch did a worthwhile thing." I looked at him over my coffee cup. "What the hell are you doing here?"

"Thought ya'll might need some help," he said.

"Now, don't come that on me. You mean *you* might need some help. What happened? Them hired hands off them ranches break you and you come running for help?"

"Now, Will," Wilcey said.

"No," I said. I was tired and cold and irritable. "We left him all the money we had and here he comes running after he's lost it. Expecting us to take him in like a long-lost brother."

Wilcey said, "You're wrong. You better wait and listen."

Well, I finally did. And after I did I was plenty ashamed.

He'd brought us twelve bottles of whiskey along with some sweet stuff that I liked so well like canned apricots and peaches and even some kind of cake.

"I don't much recommend that cake, though," he said. "Storekeeper said he'd had it about three years and wasn't even sure what kind it was."

Wilcey had opened the can and was smelling it. "Smells like it's got some kind of whiskey or rum on it."

"That's why I knew you two would like it."

He'd even brought us some new cards. Then he came out of his pocket with a sack and poured a hell of a pile of nickels on the floor. There's twenty dollars worth of nickels. I knew you two wouldn't have nothin' to bet with and I figured you'd be wanting to play a little head-up poker." He got a sly grin on his face. "My money is on Wilcey. I bet when ya'll get to town Wilcey will have every one of those nickels."

"And that ain't all, Will," Wilcey said. "Look here." He went over to the corner and came back with two coats. He pitched one to me. It was a big, heavy knee-length cowhide fleece-lined coat. It even looked warm. I caught it, looked at it, and laid it over my knees. I couldn't even look at either one of them I was so ashamed. I didn't know what to say either. Lord, I wished I'd kept my mouth shut when I'd come in.

Wilcey asked Tinhorn. "I can't understand how you come to think of these coats. We been about to freeze to death."

The Tinhorn said, "When I left out this morning I rode about a mile before I realized how cold I was. So I upped and went back to town and bought me this coat I got on. Then I got to thinking ya'll had about the same kind of clothes that I did and that you must be freezing your asses off. So I got a couple more."

"Shit!" I said, and looked at the floor. I'd like to have thought that I'd have been that thoughtful and caring about my pards, but I knew goddamn good and well I wouldn't have been. I asked, in a low voice, "How'd you know where to find us?"

"Oh," he said, "ya'll got to be well-known in a hell of a hurry. Heard you been brightening some foreman named Sawyer's life up for him. Him and a few others. Few of them hands I been playing poker with is off the Skillet Ranch and they told me how to get here."

"Pretty good ride," I said, still looking at the floor.

"Aw, I figured you two was fixing to get in trouble and I'd better come up here and straighten it out."

I finished my coffee and whiskey and got up and walked to where the canned goods were stacked. Just as I reached down to get one I said, "I ain't always a damn fool by intention. Sometimes it just happens."

They didn't say anything, but I figured they understood that was my poor way of apologizing. I got me a can of apricots, punched a hole in the top of it with my pocketknife, and poured it in my coffee cup. Then I added a pretty good shot of whiskey.

Wilcey said, "Is that still your favorite drink, Will?"

"Oh, yes," I said. I went over and sat back down on my bunk. "Either that or straight whiskey." I had a pull at the sweet juice and whiskey. Goddamn, it was good. It tasted like a craving I'd been trying to satisfy for a month. "Damn, Preacher," I said. "I could near about kiss you for this sweet stuff."

Preacher said, "Now, don't get reckless."

But I was thinking how, in just a few weeks, what a bad case of cabin fever I'd got. If I could go that loco in that short of time, what was going to happen when it stretched out to months? Here I'd almost drew down on my best friend and I misunderstood and gave a good cussing to another good friend. Hell, God knows what was liable to happen in the future.

I said, "I been feeling like a boxed-up bear."

Wilcey said, dryly, "No shit."

Preacher said, "I know the feeling. Me and another old poker-playin' buddy of mine had to hole up in a hotel room in Kansas City one time for a whole week. Easy going as we both were, we was goddamn near at gunpoint before that week was up."

"What caused you to have to hole up?" Wilcey asked curiously.

"Little gambling misunderstanding. We cheated the wrong man. Turned out he was the chief of police's brother."

Well, we went ahead and got a little serious drinking in, which made us all feel better, me especially. Then Wilcey cooked up some meat in a kind of stew and made some biscuists. Or at least he called them biscuits. I mostly called them bullets. But, then, since I couldn't cook a lick, I didn't have much room to talk. But we had that and some potatoes and then set in to drinking again.

What had happened was that the Tinhorn had got about three hundred dollars ahead. He said, "You was right, Will. Them old ranch hands can't play poker for green apples. But other than that it's been rough as hell."

"What are you talking about?"

He took a long, slow look around the shanty. "Well, having to play poker in a saloon where all they got to drink is beer and whiskey. And they ain't but two whores in town. And eatin' in them cafés that ain't got over fourteen or fifteen different things to eat. And having to sleep in a heated hotel in a bed. It's been hard."

I looked at Wilcey and he looked at me. "If we buried him in a snowdrift they wouldn't find him until spring. By then we'd be out of the country."

"Naw. He's so used to being warm. Let's tie him up in here and set the goddamn shack on fire."

It was good to be able to laugh and joke again. We had another drink and then the Tinhorn said, "By the way, Will—that man that was with the man that hired ya'll."

"Who? Gaines? The one that looks like a gunman?"

"Yeah, him. He's played in my game a couple of times. Was damn curious about you. He remembered me as being with ya'll that night. Said he'd known you somewhere's before and tried to pump me."

"What'd you tell him?"

The Tinhorn shook his head. "Nothing. I told him we'd just met up a couple of days before and that I didn't really know either one of you."

"Listen," I said, a lot of the good feeling going out of me, "you stay away from that guy. Don't have nothing to do with him if you can help it."

"Shit, I can't keep him out of my game. What do you expect?"

"Listen to Will," Wilcey said. "That guy is bad news."

"Don't cross him at all," I said. "In fact I hate to see you playing with him."

Preacher said, "Oh, he don't seem like so much."

"Look. That sonofabitch is a killer. You watch yourself around him."

After that we kind of loosened up again. We did a little more drinking and then turned in. Me and Wilcey cut cards to see who would give the Tinhorn his bed and Wilcey lost and spread his bedroll on the floor. The Tinhorn made a kind of phony protest saying he would sleep on the floor, but his heart wasn't in it. That sonofabitch knew we weren't going to make him sleep on the floor, not after all the stuff he'd brought us.

The Tinhorn stayed around a couple of extra days. The next day when Wilcey and I got in he'd even cooked supper and he turned out to be a pretty damned good cook. We'd killed a beef and we had a side hanging outside and a side hanging inside. Which will show you how cold that shanty was. That beef wouldn't freeze inside, as it would outside, but it would keep very nicely, just like in a cold box. I bet we could have kept a side all winter without it spoiling.

Anyway, the Tinhorn cut some steaks off of that and fried them up in the skillet along with some onions. He'd put on some beans early and we had that and bread and he'd even made a pudding with flour and lard and some of those canned peaches.

I told Wilcey, "Tell you what: You go on back and leave Preacher here. I tell you, I think it was about half your cooking that brought on my attack of cabin fever."

He said, that innocent look on his face, "Did you have an attack of cabin fever? I never noticed."

I gave him a sour look. "A very mild one."

We hated to see the Preacher go, but he couldn't stay on too much longer. I doubted that the Skillet Ranch would have stood for us having visitors. They probably had some regulation against it.

After he was gone we settled down to the same old routine. But we had one consolation: It was less than a week until payday and then we'd have four days off and could go to town for a little good times.

Two days before payday I finally had a little something to do about the fence. About five or six miles on out the ten-mile stretch I found about fifty yards of fence down. The wires had been cut. I couldn't make out if any cows had been either driven in or out because of the fresh snow. I started to repair the fence, then decided to come back the next day and hole up some distance away and watch to see if the gap was being used.

That evening I told Wilcey about it. He said, "Why the hell didn't you just fix the fence and forget about it?"

"I don't know," I said. "It's something to do."

Next day I found me a little shallow place in the plain about a quarter of a mile from the gap. I got there about ten of the morning, and got off my horse, and set up to watch. Well, it was a cold job, just squatting like that Fortunately it wasn't snowing and there wasn't any wind, but it would still freeze the water in your canteen. I guess, though, it was better than riding up and down that goddamn fence like a squirrel on a treadmill. God knows I didn't give a damn what happened to their drift fence. As far as I was concerned the whole damn thing could get torn down. But I did figure it would take us about four months to get ourselves in shape enough, money-wise, to pull out and I didn't want us to lose our jobs before then.

Finally, sometime after noon I saw a bunch of specks coming across the prairie. Turned out to be a little herd of cattle, maybe twenty, and three riders. I watched until they headed straight for the gap and went on through, and then I got on my horse and set out after them at a run. I was coming up from the rear and I was nearly on them before they even saw me. I got right to the herd and skidded to a stop, jerking out my rifle as I did. "Hold it!" I yelled. "Don't nobody move!"

Well, they weren't exactly dangerous-looking. It was a gaunt old man, maybe fifty years of age, and two teen-aged boys. They were probably his sons. The old man was riding a mule and nobody, as far as I could see, was armed.

They stopped and turned to face me. They didn't look scared, just sort of discouraged. You could tell they were poor by their clothes and the quality of the animals they were riding. Even the cattle looked plenty poor.

I had been covering them with my rifle, but now I dropped the barrel. Their cattle, no longer being driven, were drifting around, grazing. "Ya'll cut that fence?" I asked them.

Nobody said a word.

"Damnit! Answer me! I ain't going to hurt you."

They still just sat on their mounts and stared at me. "Don't you know you're on Skillet property?"

At that the old man roused himself up. "Be damned if that's so!" he said with some heat. "This here's state land. Open grazing land. And always has been since 'fore I come to this here country and that be thirty years ago."

"They got it leased from the state," I said.

Which roused him even more. "And be doubledamned if that be so! If they do the state ain't got no idea of it. They ain't got no right puttin' up that infernal fence!"

"So you did cut that fence."

"I ain't sayin' neither way." He gave me a look. "I guess you be one of them killers they hired to starve the rest of the folk out."

He was a skinny old man who had a prominent Adam's apple and badly needed a shave. But he didn't look too afraid of me. "Just hold up on that kind of talk," I said. "I work for the Skillet Ranch, but I ain't kilt an honest folk all day. Now, you're going to have to drive your cattle back through that gap and then get that fence back up."

The old man shook his head. "No. We damned sure won't."

I said, "Now, old man, don't give me no trouble. This fence is my job."

"No," he said again.

I looked over at the two boys. They were just ordinary-looking farm boys. I said, "Is this your daddy?"

They just stared back at me.

"What are you? Addle-brained? Answer me. Is this your paw?"

They just sat there. I turned back to the old man. "Now, look—I'm not going to give you any trouble. But you got to drive them cattle back through and fix that fence. I mean it. It's my job to see that you do."

Well, as soon as I said, "It's my job," I felt like a damn fool. God, what a sorry estate I'd fallen to. Shit, I didn't give a damn if they drove them cattle back or not.

The old man said, "They ain't got no right to have that fence there. My cattle are starving. I've got to get them to grass. They starvin' out ever' small farmer south of here. All the grass's to the north. I ain't takin' them cattle back to starve."

He just sat there looking at me like he didn't care if I shot him or not. Hell, I didn't know what to do. Here I was, armed, and they weren't. But they weren't afraid of my goddamn gun. And they weren't afraid of me.

"Listen," I said, "what the hell are ya'll's names?"

The old man wouldn't answer. Just sat there staring at me.

"Your name. God damnit, tell me your names."

"No," he said. Then he said. "We are going to drive these cattle north. If you be obliged to shoot then you go right on ahead and shoot. But we got work."

"Now just a goddamn minute—" I began. But the

old man had turned his mule, nodded at his boys, and then commenced drifting the cattle north.

Oh, shit, I thought. But I did yell after him. "Look, I'm going to repair that fence. If ya'll cut it again when you go back be sure and put the goddamn thing back. Else the company will have some men down here ain't near as charitable as I am!"

I fixed the fence, then finished my patrol and got back in that night just after dark. Wilcey and I sat and had a few drinks of whiskey while I told him what had happened. He got a good laugh out of it.

"I tell you," I said, "I never been in such fix before and I didn't know what to do. A gun ain't a goddamn bit of good if nobody's scairt of it."

"Were they just that dumb?" Wilcey asked.

I shook my head. "No. I think this country and this weather and hard times had beat them down so until they just didn't give a damn. Gettin' shot would have been the easy way out. About the only rise I got out of them was about that fence. If the rest of the nestors in this part of the country feel about that fence the way that old man does, this Skillet Ranch ain't going to be able to hire enough guns to protect it."

Wilcey kind of looked off. "I tell you, Will," he said, "I know this sounds like a mooncalf talking, but I ain't exactly pleased at myself for helpin' guard this fence. This Skillet Ranch has fenced off all the good grass, no, just about all the grass, and I imagine their intentions is to starve out these small farmers and ranchers. And these small outfits ain't hurtin' their business that bad. It's just that they be troublesome. They don't like to be cuttin' their cattle out at roundup; they don't like them choosing their cattle in with theirs. They just don't want to be bothered with them. I would bet that fence is illegal."

"It probably is," I said. "But it ain't no skin off our nose."

He looked away again. "I don't know how much more of this life I can take."

I heaved myself up and got another drink of whiskey. "Well, I just don't know what we can do about it. After payday we'll have a whole fifty dollars apiece and nowhere to go. You get any better ideas, let me know."

But I came damn near not making it to payday. Next morning we got a late start and it was good daylight before I was ready to leave. Wilcey came out to the corral where I was saddling my horse and pointed toward the northwest sky. "Sure looks like snow, Will," he said. "Look at that sky."

I looked and there was some low gray-blue clouds hanging just over the horizon. "Them's snow clouds," Wilcey said. "And they be coming this way. Looks like a real blizzard to me. You better watch yourself."

"Hell," I said, "it's just snow. And ain't we had enough of that to know what it is?"

"Listen," he said, "you ain't used to the real bad weather they get in this country. You can freeze your butt to death in one of them snowstorms before you even know it."

"Hell," I said, 'it can't get no colder than it is now." My fingers were nearly frozen stiff from trying to tie off the latigo strap on the cinch.

"Yes it can," he said. "Watch yourself."

I didn't say anything to that, though I didn't quite understand how I was supposed to watch myself against snow. I got away about half an hour later. Wilcey insisted on me taking a bottle of whiskey, though it had not been our habit to do so, along with some extra food.

He warned, "You ain't never seen a real snowstorm. You might just get that chance today."

Nothing much happened on the patrol out. In fact it didn't seem as cold as usual. I reached my turning-around point at mid-afternoon, a little later than usual because of the delayed start, and started back. Some light snow flurries had been kicking up, but I'd been seeing those nearly every day. But I did notice that it seemed to be getting darker a little earlier than usual and I noticed that that blue-gray cloud was nearly overhead. I'd been riding an hour and the wind was picking up and I was getting colder and colder. I finally pulled my horse up, dismounted, and rummaged around in my saddlebags and found the bottle of whiskey. Then I squatted in the lee of my horse, holding him by the reins, and commenced taking a few drinks of whiskey. It was snowing harder and harder and the wind was really picking up. I tried to light a cigarillo, but the wind was blowing too hard to get a match to light. About that time I commenced noticing that landscape I'd been looking at was being rapidly replaced with a white curtain of blowing snow. "The hell with this," I said aloud. I got up, took one more swig of whiskey, then plugged the bottle, put it back in the saddlebags, and swung aboard. But, in that little time, the snow had gotten so thick that I literally couldn't see five feet in front of me. When I'd pulled up I'd been riding about fifteen or twenty yards off the fence. I turned in the direction I thought it was but, after a few steps, I pulled my horse up. In that snow I wasn't going to be able to see the fence until we were right on it and I damn sure didn't want to walk my horse into a barbed-wire fence and get him cut up and go to pitching. So I got off and, taking him on lead, started walking in the direction I thought the fence was.

My Lord, it was snowing hard and thick. I could barely see my hand in front of my face. I walked for a few moments, expecting at any time to encounter the fence. No fence. After a few more minutes I was really beginning to worry. And a few minutes later I knew I was slam-ass turned around. In that blindness I barely knew up from down, much less which way was west.

"Oh, shit!" I said aloud, knowing now what Wilcey had meant about such a snowstorm. For someone who'd grown up on the border country it came as a complete surprise.

Which wasn't doing me a goddamn bit of good right then and there. For a moment I nearly panicked, but I commenced trying to get hold of myself. I was scared, scared in a way I'd never been, and make no mistake. Snow is not something you can fight with a gun. And this business of not being able to see and not knowing which direction to head out in was a new kind of scare that I'd never experienced before.

I got on my horse, taking some security from the fact that I was still mounted. I think the animal was picking up a little of my fear for he was skittish of me when I tried to mount and, even when I was in the saddle, still wanted to jump around and hump his back. I thought that all I'd need now was to get pitched off. I wouldn't last long in that cold and snow, afoot.

After I got my horse quieted down I sat a moment trying to think what to do, trying to decide which way to head. But, after a time, I realized that that was hopeless. I had no more idea about which way to head than a goose would know his manners at an inaugural ball. All I could do was pick one point of the compass out of the 360 and hope it was somewhere's in the right direction. But I did know we had to keep moving. I got my slicker off the back of the saddle and wrapped it around me as best I could. It wouldn't quite button up over my bulky jacket, but it was some protection from the cold. After that I just put my horse into a slow walk, trying to quarter off the direction of the wind in what I hoped was a generally westerly direction. If the wind had been from a constant direction I would have had some help, for it had been blowing most of the day out of the northwest. But it had commenced to swirl and jump around so that it was not to be trusted. One moment it would be cold on one cheek and a minute later blowing hard on the other. So all I could do was walk in what I hoped was a straight direction and hope it brought me to some sort of shelter.

I don't know how long we wandered. It might have been an hour, it might have been two or even three. After a time I could feel my horse begin to stumble and stagger. I didn't know if a horse could freeze to death on his feet but I was about to come of a mind that he could.

And then I got to worrying about prairie dog holes, which were all over the place. It would be very easy for him to step in one, break his leg, and leave me afoot. I'd be able to take some warmth from him before he froze to death, but I didn't think that would be long in coming.

Finally he got to stumbling so bad that I just pulled him up and sat there. If the snow had been bad while there was a little light left, it was now impossible to see at all with it pitch-black. Not only that but the contrast of the white, whirling snow in all that black was enough to make a man dizzy.

I sat there getting colder and colder, looking all around, not knowing what the hell to do. I was scared and make no mistake.

Then it seemed that I saw a little glimmer of light. I peered in the direction I thought I'd seen it, but a sudden gust of snow shut out anything I might have seen. But the next time I turned my head in that direction I was certain I'd seen some kind of light again. I kept peering, the cold and snow burning my eyes and blurring my vision. But then came a little lull and

I was certain I was seeing a speck of light. I got off my horse and began trudging in that direction, leading my animal, my eyes glued to the light that disappeared every second in the swirl of snow, afraid to even blink for fear of losing that beacon.

The light never got brighter but I bet I hadn't walked twenty feet when I bumped into something solid. It surprised me so bad I nearly dropped the reins. I tell you, it was so hard to see that it was a minute or two before I figured out that I'd bumped into a cabin and that the light I'd been seeing was from a window covered with an oilskin shade. I couldn't believe it. I'd been that goddamn close, maybe not even ten feet, and I hadn't been able to see that cabin. I felt along the wall with my hands until I found the door. Then I commenced to pound and to set up a holler. It seemed like one hell of a long time before that door was opened and then it was just a crack. A woman's voice said, "What you want?"

I said, raising my voice over the howl of the wind, "I'm lost. I'm freezing to death. Let me in!"

The door opened a little wider and, against the dimly lighted background of the cabin, I could see a gaunt, stringy-haired woman wrapped up in a man's greatcoat. "Who are you?"

Goddamn, I was freezing to death. I stamped my feet. "I work for the Skillet Ranch. Lady, I'm freezing!"

"If you work for the Skillet Ranch you kin get off my property."

She started to close the door. I shot out my hand and stopped her. I didn't try to force my way in, I just said, "Wait a minute! I don't even know where your goddamn property is! I don't even know where I am! Listen, lady, I don't know what you got against the Skillet Ranch. I only been working for them for less than a month. But I been freezing for about four hours! Now, let me in! Goddamn!"

She said, "Don't blaspheme!" But she opened the door wider. "You're not drunk, be you?"

"Oh, hell, lady! Are you crazy? Are you going to let me in?"

She opened the door wide enough for me to enter. But she said, "You mind yore manners."

I started in, but then remembered my horse. "I got a horse out here. I got to get him in shelter. Where?"

She took a moment to consider that, but then she sort of jerked her head. "Out back. They's a shed. But don't you touch none of that corn. There's precious little."

"You got a lantern, lady? Let me have that lantern just until I can put my horse up."

Well, I didn't know if she was going to do it or not. Probably thought I was going to steal her goddamn lantern. But she finally let me have it and I made my way through that still-blinding white dark as best I could until I finally stumbled onto a little shed that had a milk cow and a couple of calves in it. I led the horse in, found the corn she'd told me not to take, and gave the horse a good enough bait of it to get his blood circulating. I left the saddle and blanket on him for warmth, only loosening the cinch, and took the bridle and bits out of his mouth. He'd spend a cold night, but he wouldn't freeze. The other animals were putting out enough body warmth so that it would make the place a little warmer than the North Pole.

After that I managed to struggle my way back to the cabin. I didn't bother to knock, just shoved the door open and went inside trying to beat the snow off my clothes with my hat. The woman was sitting in a rocking chair in front of a little fireplace that was loaded with a good fire of dried cow-chips. I couldn't see nothing else but that fire. I went straight to it, taking off my coat as I did. It felt mighty warm in that cabin after the outside.

I just stood there for a long time, not saying anything, just letting that fire soak some of the chill out of my bones. I'd shoved the whiskey down in the pocket of my greatcoat and, when my hands felt like they'd warmed enough so that I could use them, I outed with the bottle and jerked the cork out with my teeth. Just as I was fixing to raise it to my lips the woman said, "You said you weren't drunk!"

I looked at her in some amazement. "Lady, I'm about to get convinced you are crazy. Ain't no way nobody could get drunk out in that storm! I'm taking a drink of this to try and save my life!" I leaned toward her, holding out the bottle. "Maybe you ought to have a drink."

She only drew her mouth up in a thin line and turned her face. "This is a Christian home," she said.

I said, "Aw, shit!" and turned the bottle up and took a long, searing drink. It took a moment, but when it hit bottom and started to spread I began to feel like I was going to live again. I had another drink, then plugged the bottle and put it back in my pocket.

Finally I began to look around. Except for some woman's touches and the fact that the lumber that made up the walls had been chinked, the cabin wasn't a whole hell of a lot different than the line shack that Wilcey and I occupied. It had a hard-packed floor and a sod roof and didn't seem to be much bigger. It did have the fireplace, which put out more heat than our little stove. Against the wall facing the door was one bed built into the wall, a bed big enough for two. It was the only bed in the cabin. In the middle was a table that had obviously been brought to the country, for it was of good quality, as were the four chairs around it. There was even a hooked rug on the floor.

In that cabin I could read that the woman had probably come to the Panhandle from a more civilized place, probably to get married, and she'd brought her dowry along with her in the form of some furniture her family had probably given her. Her husband could have been away, but I didn't see the slightest sign of a man about the place: no gun, no tools, and no clothes. I figured she was probably a widow woman. Though why she'd have wanted to stay on in such a place if she'd lost her man was a hell of a lot more than I could figure out.

I said to her, "My name is Wilson. I'm new to this country and new to this kind of weather. I'm sorry to barge in on you like this, but I sure do appreciate you taking me in. I was near about to die out there in that storm."

She sort of pushed her hair back with her hand and said, without looking at me, "Don't matter. I'd of taken in a dog on a night like this. Even if the dog worked for the Skillet Ranch."

I just let that pass. I'd figured out the small farmers and ranchers weren't too kindly disposed toward the Skillet and I didn't want to get into any discussions that might get me thrown out.

"For whatever reason," I said. "I'm grateful."

My eyes were starting to unblur a little from what the cold had done to them and I could see the woman better. At first I'd thought she was old, but, now, I could see that she wasn't much over thirty. She looked work-worn and used-up, but I could almost see where, at one time, she'd have been thought of as pretty. Her face was thin, but it wasn't gaunt; she had kind of stringy, light-brown hair, but it probably would have been pretty if it was fixed up. Her hands were delicately shaped, though you could see they were red and rough from hard usage. Of course I couldn't tell much about her body, not swaddled up as she was in the man's greatcoat. But what I noticed most about her were her eyes—that and the tone of her voice. It was that same deadness I'd seen in the old man and his two sons. Plain, slam-ass give-upness. But I reckoned enough of that Panhandle country would do that to you.

I said, "Your husband out?"

She said, in a dull voice, pushing her hair back from one side of her face as she'd done before, "I'm a widow. My husband died near eight months ago."

I said, "Oh."

We went on in silence for a few more minutes, me standing in front of the fireplace, her sitting in her rocking chair.

"Wonder what time it is?" I finally asked.

"I ain't got no timepiece," she finally said.

"I lost track of time in that storm. And I couldn't see the moon. But I'd reckon it to be late."

"Yes. I was in bed when yore knock came. Reckon I'll go back."

I asked, as politely as I knew how, "Wonder where I could sleep? If you had an extra quilt I could make out here on the floor."

"No," she said. "No, I ain't got no extra cover. Reckon we'll have to bundle." She got up out of the chair and went to the bed, taking off the robe as she did. She was wearing a woolen nightgown. She got into bed, shrugging in under the covers, and moving to the side next to the wall. I just stood there, not quite sure what I ought to do. She sort of raised up her head and looked at me. "Well, come on!"

"Uh," I said. "Well, uh—well, all right." I went over to the bed and sat down on the side and took my boots off. Then I sort of started to lean back on the edge, meaning to stay as far away from her as I could for fear that I might frighten her. Bundling was a common enough custom, I'd heard, in cold country, but it was my first crack at it and I wasn't sure what a body was supposed to do.

She said, "You'll have to take yore clothes off. They are dirty and smelly and I don't want 'em in my bed."

Well, that made sense to me. The lantern was on the table, still ablaze. I got up and blew it out. But the fireplace was still putting out enough light that you could dimly see. I went ahead and shucked my shirt and then took off my pants. I was wearing long-handled underwear, but it was still my underwear. I ain't normally shy about women, but this woman reminded me more of somebody's old maid schoolteacher sister and I wasn't exactly used to undressing in front of that kind. But I went ahead and got down to my long-handles. As quick as I could I slid in under the covers. She said, "You don't smell so good yourself. I reckon it wasn't just your clothes. By rights you ought to take a tub bath, but I'll let it pass. So be it, so be it."

I didn't say anything. I figured the woman had been living too long by herself and was touched. I got under the cold covers, waiting for them to warm up. The bed wasn't as wide as it had looked, but I was staying as far over to the edge as I knew how. The last thing I wanted to do was to scare her or to make her think I was making improper advances. All I wanted to do was stay out of that storm for the night and then make it back to camp the next day.

I was so tired I was having trouble going to sleep. Plus I was kind of holding myself stiff, afraid I might slip over too far and touch her. But, after a time, I figured she was asleep and I kind of relaxed and spread myself. I was kind of starting to doze when I felt her move closer to me. I was lying on my back and it felt like she was on her side facing me. First she commenced to kind of moan, real low. So low at first that I could barely hear it. Then, as she got louder she began to move closer until she was clung right up to me. "*Oooooooh,*" she was saying, "*Ooooooooh. Oooooooh. Oooooooooooh!*"

Then she said, still in that kind of moan, "It's been so long. *Soooooo loooooong.*"

At first I thought she was asleep and dreaming about her dead husband. I said, "Lady—"

But she wasn't asleep. She was awake and knew what she was doing. She said, "Don't talk. No. *Oooooooooh.*"

Good God, I didn't know what to think, much less what to do. Then she flung an arm over me and began squeezing me around the chest. "It's been *soooo loooong.*"

"Lady—" I began again, but she wasn't having any of it. I could feel her moving around under the covers and then I realized she was pulling up her gown when my hand touched her bare thigh. Now there was no mistaking her intentions. Next thing I knew she was clawing at the buttons of my long-handles. "*Hurrrrrrry!*" she was kind of moaning. "*Hurrrry! Hurry! Soooo long.*"

Well, I didn't know what to say. Goddamn, I ain't adverse to a piece of ass, but this was the last event I would have expected to happen this night and it had thrown me so off guard I wasn't sure if I could perform. There wasn't the slightest doubt in my mind that she wanted me to fuck her. But, hell, I didn't know if I could. I'd been nearly frozen to death, I was tired as hell, and she was about the strangest woman I'd ever found myself in bed with.

Finally I thought, well, like a mule, I can try. So I pulled her fingers away from the buttons of my long-handles, unbuttoned them myself, got out of the underwear, and turned to her.

Well, I've been with a lot of women in my life and if she wasn't the most passionate she was damn well gaining on the leaders. From the moment I entered her she turned me everyway but loose, all the time almost smothering me with wide-mouthed wet kisses. That woman had a head of steam up in her boiler like you wouldn't have believed. Not only did she make me perform, she made me perform several times in a row—something I hadn't been able to do for a long time.

And then it was suddenly over for her. When it was she pushed me off her and, without a word, scooted away and closed her eyes and was almost instantly asleep. I was still in a state of astoundment. For a few minutes I lay on my side, my head propped up on my hand. Then I lifted the blanket and looked down at her body. She had a surprisingly good figure with nice firm breasts and her skin was white and smooth. I let the covers back down and just shook my head. Women have generally fooled me, but never quite as bad.

She was already up when I awoke the next morning. For a moment I watched her bustling between her stove and the little table. Her hair was still stringy, but now she'd tied it back with a ribbon and it made her face look more cheerful. Also younger. She still had on the man's greatcoat and the same pair of work shoes she'd worn the night before, but now I knew what was under that coat.

She noticed I was awake. "Git up and warsh," she said. "Breakfast is nigh ready." She jerked her head toward the corner. "They's water in that pail."

I threw back the covers and started out of bed. Naturally I hadn't put my underwear back on. She threw her hands in front of her face and whirled her back to me. "Goshen! Ain't you got no shame? Cover yourself!"

So we were back to Sunday school. I just shook my head wearily and got dressed. She kept her back to me the whole time. When I had my boots and hat and gunbelt on I said, "Okay, you can turn around, September Morn."

She went on with her chores like I wasn't even in the room. I went over to the pail and rinsed my mouth out and washed my face and hands. After that I went and sat down at the table and she brought me coffee, or what she had for coffee. Actually it was parched wheat that you might think tastes like coffee if you ain't never drank coffee. But I had already figured she was probably having a hard time of it and damn well couldn't afford coffee. It was still plenty cold in the cabin, but not so cold as it would have been if she hadn't gotten up and lit a fire. I got my bottle of whiskey out and poured some in the wheat coffee. It helped the flavor considerably.

After I'd drunk my coffee she brought me breakfast. It wasn't much—fried salt pork and biscuits—but I figured it was the best she had. The biscuits were good and I ate several. "Ain't you going to eat?" I asked her. She was hovering around behind me with the coffee pot.

"I'll wait 'till you et."

"For God's sake, sit down," I said. "You make me nervous back there like that."

But she wouldn't do it.

I asked, "Has it stopped snowing yet?"

"Purty nearly," she said. "But the drifts are high."

At one point she said, "Name's Hester. Hester Godchaux. You might have knowed my husband, Amos Godchaux."

"I ain't from around here," I said. She was standing just to my left. I looked at her, her body lost in the bigness of that man's coat. Then I reached out and touched where her breast was. She immediately slapped my hand.

"Mind yore manners!"

"Why, you didn't mind yours last night."

She blushed scarlet and turned away. I laughed. "What's the matter, Hester? Have you already forgotten?"

"You're a cad," she said.

Hell, I didn't believe I'd ever been called a cad before. I got up and went up behind her and put my arms around her middle and drew her to me. But she immediately began to struggle so I let her go.

"Keep yore hands to yorself!" she said, and ran over to the fire and made herself busy. I laughed again and went to the door and opened it and looked out. It had cleared off and was some warmer, the wind having layed, but there was a power of snow on the ground. I stepped out, closing the door behind me, and trudged out to the shed to see about my horse. He was all right, as was the milk cow and the two calves. They were contentedly sucking away, though one looked big enough to have been weaned. The old mama cow kept kicking at him, trying to drive him away, but he wanted to get to that teat so he was a little hard to discourage.

I knew just how he felt.

I fed my horse a few more ears of corn, noting just how few she had left. Well, I was going to do something about her situation.

I went on back in the house. She'd got a straw broom and was sweeping the hearth. All the money I had was a pocketful of nickels from playing poker with Wilcey the night before. I got them out and piled them on the table. I didn't figure there were more than three or four dollars worth.

"Hester, that's all the money I got with me, but—"

She said, "Ain't no call you to be leavin' no money."

"Look," I said, "I want to leave it. I wish I had more. You may not know it but you saved my cornbread ass last night from—"

"Please don't blaspheme!"

"The hell with that," I said. She was still standing over by the fireplace. I was buttoning up my coat with the intention of leaving. "Let me ask you a little something." She didn't say anything so I went on. "What the hell are you doing here? What have you got here? All I see is a milch cow and two calves. That and a sod-roofed house and a lot of snow."

She got that vague look on her face. "Well, Amos had two sections. And we got twenty or thirty cattle scattered somewhere. And I got that cow. And the corn crop came in after Amos died and I got it in."

"Listen, where the hell you from? I mean, where did you come from before you come to this godforsaken place?"

"Oh, Texas. East Texas. Jefferson. Mister Godchaux came through there two years ago. I'm barren, don't you know. He was always reminding me of that. Can't have children. I thought I'd keep his place. I ain't got nowheres else to go."

"Oh, the hell with this," I said. Goddamn, of all the foolish women I'd ever known, and I'd known plenty, she took the cake. I went over and give her a little shake. "Hester," I said. "Hester!"

She finally looked me in the eye.

"I'll be back. Maybe this evening if it don't commence to snow again. Now, come outside and tell me where I am."

"What?"

I didn't try to talk to her then. I just took her by the arm and led her outside. "Now, tell me where that Skillet fence is. I bet you know where that is."

"Oh," she said. "It's just north of here. About two or three miles. You can't miss it. You'll ride right into it."

"All right, Hester," I said. "You go on back in the house and get warm."

I went on in the cowshed and saddled my horse and led him up to the front door. When I went inside she was back in her rocking chair, just rocking and staring into the now low flames of the cow-chips.

"Hester," I said, "I'm going. But I'll be back."

"Of course you will," she said, back in that vague voice. "Just like Mister Godchaux."

"Yes," I said. I went over and bent down and kissed her on the lips. Then I turned without another word and went outside and mounted my horse and rode away.

I went north for about an hour, struck the fence as she'd said, and then turned west. Two hours later I was back at the line camp. I hadn't been that far away the whole time, maybe six or seven miles as the crow flies.

I turned my horse into the corral, fed him, and then went on inside. Wilcey was asleep sitting up on his bunk, fully clothed with a blanket wrapped around his shoulders.

I clumped on in as quiet as I could, found me some cold beef, for I was still hungry, and broke out a new bottle of whiskey. Then I sat down on my bunk and commenced to eat and drink. He just sat there sleeping, his back propped up against the cabin wall, with his hat and spurs on. I never said a word but, I reckon, he gradually became aware of my presence. Finally his eyes flickered open and he said, "Shit, where you been?"

I was chewing a mouthful of beef and it took me a minute to answer. Then I said, "I been to the dance downtown."

He still wasn't awake, but he said, "You sonofabitch. I been waiting all night for your ass. Figured you was frozen. Couldn't get out last night on account of the snow. Figured I'd wait until the morning when it cleared off and then go find yore stiff carcass in a snowdrift somewheres. Damn border outlaw, don't know nothing about snow country."

"Well, go ahead," I said. "I ain't really here. You're still asleep and you just dreamin' all this."

But he was starting to rouse. "Aw, fuck you," he said. "I'm disappointed as hell you ain't froze solid." Then he spied the whiskey. "Throw me that," he said.

I pitched him the bottle.

After he'd had a good pull he finally kind of sat up and looked at me. "What the hell happened to you?"

I shook my head. "If I was to tell you, you still wouldn't believe me."

"Try me," he said.

I figured he was awake enough by then so I went ahead and told him the whole story. When I was through he just sat there staring at me for a long minute. Then he said, "God damnit, Young, I've known old boys who couldn't get fucked in a whorehouse with a thousand dollars cash in their pockets, but you are the only sonofabitch I know could find a piece of ass in a snowstorm!"

"Now, wait a minute," I said. "That ain't the point."

But he was still just looking at me, shaking his head. "I tell you. You got me beat to the wide. I never seen a man could run up on to so many complications with women as you can. I ain't going to be surprised at what happens next."

"Listen, she's a nice lady. Just been livin' by herself too long."

"Yeah," he said, that dry tone in his voice.

"Hadn't been for her I'd of froze to death."

He said, "Shelter is one thing."

"Now, watch that."

Well, neither one of us rode fence that day. We reckoned the Skillet Ranch could afford it. It stayed clear with no more prospects of a blizzard in view so, about early afternoon, I started loading two of the horses with a quantity of supplies. I loaded up two hundred pounds of grain for her stock, and about fifty pounds of flour and a good quantity of coffee and what sugar we could spare and some lard and some of our canned goods. Wilcey watched me with a sour expression on his face. "Moving out?"

"Now, don't complain. I'm takin' her the soap which I knowed has been a bother to you, it laying around here reminding you you ought to take a bath."

"Shit," he said.

Then I took the side of beef we had frozen outside. I didn't figure she'd killed a beeve, not judging from that fried salt pork I'd eaten.

Wilcey said, "We'll have to kill another one. And this time, by God, you're going to butcher it."

"I'm going to take about five dollars of these nickels," I told him.

He gave me that sour look. "How about my cigarillos? Does she smoke? Maybe you'd like to take our whiskey along in case she drinks."

When I was loaded I saddled up and swung in the saddle, taking the two packhorses on lead. "Don't look for me home early, mother," I said.

"Go to hell," was all he said.

I pointed the horses to the south and slightly southeast. The snow was still pretty heavy, but the wind was starting to pick up and was blowing it so that it would be gone pretty soon. I made it to her place with plenty of daylight left. The sky was staying clear so I wasn't anticipating a storm. At least not outside.

When I got there I pulled up by her front door, with no sign from inside, and off-loaded the goods that were to go in the house. Then I took the three horses out to the shed, got them unpacked and unsaddled, and fed them and the milk cow and the two calves.

There was still no sign from the house as I trudged up there. I didn't bother to knock, just got me an armload of stuff and commenced carrying it in. She was sitting in front of the fireplace, just watching the flames. She give a big start as I came in and flung her hand over her mouth.

"It's only me," I said, bringing the stuff in and stacking it against the far wall.

"Oh," she said. "What are you doing here?"

"Another storm," I said. I went on back outside and brought in another load. I'd considered what to do with the side of beef. It was a touch too warm in the cabin to keep it there, but it was still frozen enough for the time being so I lugged it on in.

"What is all this?" she asked me. She was standing in front of the fireplace, running her hands down the front of that big coat she was wrapped up in like a woman will run her hands down the front of her apron.

"What does it look like?" I asked her, a growl in my voice because I was just a touch embarrassed.

"But I can't let you do this," she said.

I sat down at the table and propped my feet up in a nearby chair. "You can't? Then why don't you try and stop me."

"Oh, my," she said. "Oh, my, oh, my!" She turned away and put her hands over her face.

"Listen," I said, "I'm damned tired and hungry from packing this stuff over here. Now, can you cook? Or has it been so long that you've forgotten?"

She was still faced away from me with her hands in front of her face.

I said, "In case you can, I want you to carve me a beefsteak off that side over there in the corner and fry it. And I want you to make me some biscuits and I want you to make me some real coffee. I mean real coffee. You reckon you can do that?"

WILSON'S CHOICE

She didn't answer for a long moment and I thought I might have overplayed my hand with my gruff voice. But then came a little quick nod of her head.

"All right," I said. "Get about it. I'm gonna sit here with my feet up and drink whiskey and smoke cigarillos."

She moved very hesitantly at first, like a little puppy unsure of her ground. First she kind of looked at the side of beef then she went to the sack of flour and opened it. She still had her back to me, but I could see her dip her hands into the flour. Then she went to the sack of coffee and kind of leaned down and smelled it. I saw her give me a quick look just before she picked up one of the cans I'd brought and examined it.

"Say," I called to her, "do you know how to make hounds' ears and whirlips?"

Then she did turn around and look at me, giving a quick little nod.

"Then make them," I said. "And use the canned peaches. That's my preference."

She turned away and I said, "And bring me one of them cans of apricots and a tin cup."

She brought it over, but she wouldn't look at me, wouldn't meet my eyes. I took the tin cup and the can of apricots, opened the can and poured the juice in the cup and then added whiskey from the bottle I'd brought. Then I sat back, sipping at it.

All of a sudden Hester turned to me. "Mister Wilson—"

Hell, she'd remembered my name.

"Mister Wilson, would you be good enough to go and see about the stock?"

I was a little perplexed. "Hell," I said, "I done seen about 'em. I told you I fed the whole bunch."

"Please, Mister Wilson. I don't believe I watered the stock. There is a water trough right beside the windmill, behind the shed. I don't believe I broke the ice on it. And it will freeze again tonight. Would you do that?"

"Hell," I said, "the stock ain't going to want to drink tonight. I'll do it in the morning."

"No, please do me this boon."

I looked at her, kind of puzzled. She looked so anxious. "Well, all right," I said. I drained off the last of my syrup and whiskey drink, got into my coat and went out the door. I couldn't figure out why the goddamn woman got so anxious, all of a sudden, about the stock. But that was a woman for you.

It was just coming twilight. If anything, since the norther had blowed itself out, it was getting warmer. Or at least it felt that way, which was all that mattered.

I found the watering trough, a big, round wooden sink set in the ground that fed off a pipe from the windmill. One thing was sure in this country: They weren't ever going to have problems gettin' a windmill to work.

There was only skim ice on top, which I'd figured, the way the sun had been shining down all afternoon. But I found a stick and stirred it up pretty good. After that I saw to the horses and the cow and her calves. They were doing fine except the cow was still having trouble kicking the weaned bull-calf loose from her teat.

I still knew how he felt. Hell, what was I doing where I was if not the same thing?

After that I hunkered down out of the wind and smoked a cigarillo and looked out at the horizon. I had the whiskey bottle in the pocket of the big coat ol' Tinhorn had bought me and I outed with that and had a pretty good pull.

Hell, I tell you the truth, I was feeling pretty contented. My efforts for the day done, a good drink of whiskey in my belly, a good smoke, supper getting ready on the table, a good woman for bed later on that night.

I didn't want much else than that.

I finally went on back in the cabin. As soon as I got back in I saw why she'd wanted me to go tend to the stock. She'd, in the little time I'd given her, fixed herself up. She'd taken off that big coat and those work shoes and put on what women call a housedress. She tied her hair back with a ribbon again and she'd even rouged her cheeks. But she was bustling around at the stove like she didn't want me to notice.

"Mister Wilson," she said, severely. "Jest sit down at the table, if you're a mind. And let me get this done. Lands! So much to do!"

I sat down at the table, watching her, almost grinning. She was bustling about, cooking supper once again for a man and I could see the pleasure she took of it in every movement of her body. When she put the steak on I could hear her mumbling under her breath, "Oh, this won't be right! He won't like it. Oh, the biscuits!"

Then she'd spring to the side to stir up her biscuit batter. And then, "Oh, lands! The coffee is going to boil over!"

Pretty soon she turned around to me, and this time she did have on an apron to wipe her hands down the front of. "Mister Wilson, would you take a coffee first?"

"Yeah," I said. "What's holding up supper?"

"Well, I'm doing the best I can, ain't I?"

I tell you, it was mighty cozy in that cabin with the supper fire burning and a lantern for light and all that cold outside. And me with a hot cup of coffee brought to me that I laced with whiskey. Just sitting there with my boots up on a chair and taking my ease.

Then, all of a sudden she said, with a kind of half-catch in her voice, "Oh, I never thought. Mister Wilson, do you take milk in yore coffee?"

I wasn't thinking. I said, "When I can get it."

I was faced away from her. Next thing she was putting on that big coat again, "Oh, goddamn!" I said. "Let's don't go back to that!"

"If you please," she said. And next thing she was out the door.

I couldn't figure it. I figured the goddamn woman had gone out of her head again. I just sat back, sipping at my coffee and whiskey and shaking my head. But before I knew it she was back, carrying a little tin pail. Then she was coming over with a pitcher and pouring some milk in my coffee. Goddamn, if she hadn't gone out and milked the cow enough for something for my coffee. It made me laugh out loud. I said, "I bet that made the bull-calf mad."

"What's that you say, sir?"

"Nothing," I said. "Thanks." But I was still laughing.

I tell you the pleasure it give me watching the pleasure she was getting from doing things for a man again was a thing to enjoy. I'd come in that cabin and she'd been wrapped up in that big coat, staring into the fire, and now she was up and bustling around with rouge on her cheeks and it seemed like she was a different woman.

Then she brought my supper. First she brought me over a steak that was just a little too big for the plate. Then she brought over a platter of biscuits and set them down in the middle of the table. I sat there looking at it while she was pouring me some fresh coffee. Then I took up my knife and fork and cut that steak in two.

"Hester," I said, not waiting for her to answer, "bring another plate."

"What?"

"Bring another plate!"

Which she did. I took my fork and put half that steak on the plate she'd brought and then I pointed at the chair opposite me. "Sit down," I said.

It took her up short. "Oh, I couldn't!"

"I bet you can," I said. I got up and escorted her around the table. Then I pulled her chair out and sat her down. In that instant I loved her face, the look that was on it. I took her by the chin and gently turned her up to me and kissed her lips.

"Oh, my!" she said.

Then I went around the other side and sat down and commenced eating.

I kept my eyes down because I could tell she felt a little strange, but pretty soon she got to eating and I could tell that that beefsteak tasted mighty good to her after that salt pork she'd been eating.

It took us awhile but when we were finished I said, "Now, woman, where's them hounds' ears and whirlips you promised me?"

She got up just as prim as you could imagine. "If you'll just give me a minute. The batter is all ready. And it won't take a minute to make the whirlips."

She was busy for a few minutes and then asked me, kind of hesitantly, "Mister Wilson, how do you know about hounds' ears and whirlips?"

"What's that?" I asked her.

She still had her back to me. "I mean, you are not a ranch hand. And this is something for ranch hands."

Hounds' ears and whirlips is a chuck wagon dish of a kind of fried batter with a sauce made of canned peaches or apricots, or what have you, poured over it. I had heard that a cook could be dirty or a thief or too much of a talker but, if he could make hounds' ears and whirlips, he was able to get by with almost anything.

I said, "What makes you ask such a tomfool question?"

She said, "My husband, Mister Godchaux, was a drover before I married him. It was him requested this dish."

I said, "How you know I wasn't a drover?"

She turned around and looked at me, looking kind of helpless. "'Cause I don't think you are, Mister Wilson. Not the way you have that big pistol on yore hip."

I didn't say anything.

She said, "Mister Wilson, what is it you do?"

I still didn't say anything.

She said, "I know you ride for that fence, don't you? I've heered they've hired a bunch of bad men to make sure nobody gits near that fence. You be one of them, don't you?"

I glanced at her face. She looked what I'd have called all upset.

I said, "Look here, what if I was to tell you the truth? What would you do with it?"

She was grinding her hands in her apron. "I know I ain't got no right. I ought not to be askin' you these things."

"Then let it be," I told her.

"But, Mister Wilson, you ain't nothing like a cowhand. You ain't nothing like my Amos. I don't know what to think. Are you one of that fence gang?"

I got a little angry about then. "Listen," I said, "I ain't of no gang. I done told you I been in this country a very short time. And I been working for that ranch a very short time. Now, would you let it lay? I'm feeling pretty pleasant right now; I'd appreciate it if you wouldn't get me bothered."

Well, she looked at me a long time and then she said, back in that kind of busy housewife's way, "Mister Wilson, would you mind taking that tub that's in the corner yonder and fillin' it with snow?"

I looked over in the corner. It was one of them long tubs that people bathe in, though not as long as the ones you'd see in a bathhouse. I kind of shrugged. "Reckon so," I said. I got it up and went out the door. It was good and dark now and plenty cold. I packed the tub just as tight as I could with snow before it melted down to almost nothing. When I took it back in she directed me to set it in front of the fire so that it would melt.

"And that bucket yonder and bring in more snow as it melts down."

Well, that was better than answering questions about my livelihood, so I did as she asked. The snow, in front of that hot fire, was melting about as fast as I could bring it in. After about four loads the tub had a good sight of water in it and she said, "That be enough and yore hounds' ears and whirlips is ready."

So I sat back down at the table while she brought me the dessert and a fresh cup of coffee.

Well, it was about as good as I'd eaten. I know it's strange for a grown man to have the kind of sweet tooth I have, but I'd always had it. I think it came from eating so much dried beef. Meat had always been the staple of my diet, but a regular bait of that leaves you with a craving for something else and mine had always gone toward sweets and raw vegetables.

But, hell, I couldn't complain. As a matter of fact I couldn't remember being sick a day in my life. Hurt, wounded, yes, but not sick, like some old lady.

I noticed she was heating a kettle of water in the fireplace. Then, pretty soon, she strung a rope line across the room in front of the fireplace.

"What the hell you doing, woman?" I asked her.

"I be going to take a bath," she said, "with some of this good soap you brung me."

Well, that was fine with me. I like a sweet-smelling female.

After a time she got her a blanket and draped it across the line so that it hid the fireplace area from the rest of the room. That made me kind of grin. She was getting modest again.

I said, "Hester, you know I done seen you. What you need to put up that blanket for?"

She said, "You mind yore manners, mister."

I laughed. In a minute she called me to come pour the kettle of boiling water in the tub. She was standing there, looking prim in her housedress. When I got the water poured I asked her, "Want me to wash your back?"

"Now, you get out of here, sir," she said. "And don't you peek, neither."

"Wouldn't think of it," I said.

I went back and sat down at the table, enjoying the coffee and whiskey and feeling mighty content in that warm cabin with a pretty good-looking female getting herself ready for me. I thought of old Wilcey back at our line-camp cabin eatin' cold food and fighting the drafts whistling through them walls. He was probably hunched up before our little stove with a blanket around his shoulders. It made me grin.

Well, I went on sitting there, enjoying myself, and pretty soon she called me. I went around the edge of the blanket and she was standing there in a woolen robe, looking flushed from her bath.

"Now, sir, it's yore turn," she said.

"What do you mean, my turn?"

"For a bath. Take yore clothes off."

"The hell you say! I ain't taking no bath!"

"Yes, you are, sir. I've got some water heating in the kettle and it'll be ready about the time you git yore clothes off."

I stared at her. "Now, wait a minute. You strung that blanket up for yourself. And now you intend for me to take my clothes off in front of you?"

"Yes, sir. I'm going to give you a good scrubbing."

"Be goddamn if that's so. How come I didn't give you a good scrubbing?"

"That, sir," she said, "is different. Now, begone with your clothes. The kettle is coming to a boil."

I just stared at her, but while I was staring I took off my hat and gunbelt and then sat down in her rocking chair and pulled off my hat and my boots. Then I took off my shirt and pants.

She said, "Now, before you get down naked, get up and pour this kettle of water up."

I did as she told me. I tell you, she was about the goddamndest woman I'd ever known. Then, as if she were making shooing motions to a bunch of chickens, she said, "Now, hurry, before the water gets cold."

So I took off my long-handles. She didn't pay me any more mind than if I were a fence post.

"Git in the tub," was all she said.

I got in and, my, it did feel pretty good. I hadn't sunk my body down in a tub of hot water in a long time.

Well, she got just as busy as you please. Next thing I knew she was coming at me with that cake of soap and just fairly making the lather fly.

"Take it easy, god damnit!" I said. "You're about to take the hide off."

But she didn't pay me any mind. "I'm going to give you a good warshing. I swear, some of that dirt is an inch thick. You just behave yourself and set still."

Well, she scrubbed me all over. And I mean all over. She even soaped up my private parts, which caused me to become aroused, but she didn't pay any more attention to that than if I was a lump of clay. When she'd soaped me and rinsed me about what seemed a dozen times she stepped back and said, "Now, sir, git out of the tub."

I got out and she came at me with a big woolen cloth and dried me off.

I asked her, "Did Amos put up with this foolishness?"

"Men ain't got no sense about some things," she said firmly. "And a woman has to take a strong hand."

When I was dry I started toward my clothes, but she said, "Do not touch those filthy things."

Then she snatched up my clothes, unloading the pockets first, and flung them in the bath water.

"I'll wash these out and then hang them up to dry tonight and you'll have fresh to put on of a morning."

Hell, she had it all figured out.

But I asked, "What the hell am I supposed to wear in the meantime?"

Which put a kind of shy look on her face. "You won't need none," she said. "Now, you go on to bed and I'll be along directly."

I didn't need much more of an invitation. I went on around that blanket, picking up that bottle of whiskey as I did so, and slid between them covers.

Well, she was a good deal longer coming to bed than I wanted her to be. But she finally came around that blanket. The lamp was still burning on the table and she paused to blow it out. She was wearing a kind of woolen robe over her nightgown. But when she crawled across me to get to her side of the bed she wasn't wearing anything.

From out of them covers that woman came to me, her bare skin to mine. And it wasn't as it had been the night before, when she'd needed me so bad. Now it seemed that she was dead set on pleasing me. And, for a lady I'd thought of as a Sunday-school teacher, she sure did a hell of a good job.

When it was over I kind of lay on my back and thought about her, thought about my feelings toward her. Hell, tell you the truth I felt *fonder* toward her than I reckon I'd ever felt in my life toward any woman. She was so goddamn giving and man-pleasing.

And I hadn't run on to many of that kind. Most of what I'd known had been trying to count your poke down and see what you were worth.

But not this one.

We lay there on our backs. I reckon we stared up at the ceiling for a bit of time. Finally I heard her kind of cough. I put my hand over her. "You're a hell of a woman," I said.

She kind of turned over and buried her face in my shoulder. "You feel so good, Mister Wilson."

I don't know. For some reason it made me angry. I raised up in the covers. I said, "Listen, woman, my last name is not Wilson. Wilson is my first name. My whole name is Wilson Young, and I'm about to get tired of not being able to say it."

She sat up, looking kind of startled. "I don't understand you, sir."

"Well, I'm fixing to make you understand me. You been dying to know who I am and what I do and now I'm just going to tell you."

She kind of sat up and looked at me. I said, "You been talking about how friendly that revolver and I are and there's a damn good reason for that. For a number of years that side-gun has been my best friend. Whether you are going to like it or not, I'm a well-known outlaw and killer."

She kind of dragged her breath in when I said that.

I said, "I'm about as wanted by the law as a man can get. Me and my partners got down on our luck out in California and we come up here because it was about the only place I could think of that they ain't somebody looking for us. You were dead right about that when you said I didn't seem like no drover or ranch hand. That I ain't. I'm only riding this fence because it gives us a little money and a place to hide out in. But I don't give a good goddamn about that Skillet Ranch or their goddamn fence. As far as I'm concerned, when we leave, anybody that wants to can tear the goddamn thing down. In fact I may tear some of it down myself."

She was sort of sitting up in bed, staring down at me, her hand over her heart.

I glanced up at her. "Now you understand?"

"Oh, my," she said, "Oh, my. Oh, my!"

Then she immediately crawled across me and got out of bed and went groping around and lit the lantern. Then she took the blanket down and commenced wringing out my clothes.

"Hester," I said.

"I've got to get these here clothes done," she said. "They need to get hung on the line while the fire's still up so they'll be dry by the morning."

"Hester," I said, "god damnit, did you hear what I just told you?"

"Oh, my," she said. "Oh, my yes!"

"Then how can you be doing clothes at a time like this?"

"Because they need it," she said.

I just shook my head. "Oh, god damnit!"

I watched her for awhile and then sat up in bed. The cabin was warm enough that it was comfortable without any cover on. I said, "Any of that coffee left?"

She finished wringing out my britches and said, "They be a little. I'll fetch you a cup. And they's still some cow's milk."

"And hand me that bottle of whiskey."

She brought it over and I laced up the cup of coffee with whiskey and then sat there watching while she finished wringing out my clothes and hanging them on the line.

"There," she said, stepping back.

"Hester," I said, "I don't quite get you."

"How is that?"

"After what I told you you went over and started washing clothes. Without a word."

"The clothes needed warshing," she said.

"I know. You told me that. But right then? Right after I just got through telling you I was a killer and a robber?"

She didn't say anything.

I said, "Well, what are you going to do with what I just told you?" I was already beginning to have a little twinge of worry about shooting my mouth off. I didn't really know this woman. What if she went to the sheriff or, worse, to the Skillet Ranch?

She looked up at me. "What do you be meaning?"

"I mean they might be a reward out for me. What are you going to do with what you know about me?"

She looked puzzled. "I don't quite understand you, Mister Wilson. I ain't gonna do nothin'. You mean, would I try to hurt you?"

"Something like that," I said.

She still looked puzzled. "Why would I want to do you harm? Ye been nothing but kind to me and it's been a spell since anybody was kind to me the way you've been. I don't wish you nothin' but the best."

Well, she shamed me pretty good and no mistake. "Aw, shit," was all I could say. I looked away.

We went to sleep not much later with not too many more words being passed. I reckon the last thing I thought about her was that she was the most different woman I'd ever known.

She was up before me again next morning. When I came awake just before first light she already had the coffee on and was fixing me some flapjacks and some of the bacon I'd brought.

"I ain't got no long sweetenin'," she said by way of excuse for not having any syrup. "But I could pour you some of them canned peaches over the hot cakes if that would suit you."

"Sounds all right to me," I said. She'd had a fire built long enough so that the cabin was warm. I got up and sat at the table and smoked a cigarillo and drank the cup of coffee she brought me. All I put on was a blanket over my nakedness but, this morning, she didn't say a word about it. She was wearing her woolen robe over her nightdress. I didn't know when she'd put the gown on for she'd been naked when I'd gone to sleep. Sometime during the night I reckoned.

I only brought it up one time about what I'd told her the night before. I said, "Hester, what I told you is pretty serious. I hope you realize the trouble it could make me and my partner."

She said, "I done told you what I think about that. Onliest thing it makes me feel is that you don't like that fence. That fence is starving folks out in this south part of the range."

"We'll get something done about it," I said.

She had baked up a power of biscuits for me to take back. I'd told her about Wilcey and his biscuits and she'd done it before I was even awake. I reckoned there was six dozen biscuits in the old flour sack she had them done in.

After breakfast I went to the shed and saddled my horse and then led him back to the cabin. She was waiting at the door. She handed me the biscuit sack and I tied it on my saddle.

"When you be back?" she asked me.

I said, "We're getting paid and then we'll be going into town. Probably be four or five days. Can I bring you anything from town?"

She shook her head real quick. Hell, she almost

looked like she was going to cry. I kissed her. "You take care, Hester. I'll be back."

She looked miserable, like she didn't believe I'd be back. "I'll be back," I said again.

"You're a good man, Mister Young. I'll be waiting for you."

I kissed her again and then swung into the saddle. " 'Bye. I'll see you pretty soon."

Then I swung my horse around, put him in a lope, and went on off across the prairie. It was a clear, cold day.

Chapter Four

A little after dawn on payday me and Wilcey took off for the ranch headquarters. We met our two replacements, regular ranch hands, about ten miles west, but we didn't do much more than nod and give a howdy. I don't reckon they cared too much for our kind.

It was plenty cold, but we both felt good getting away from that line cabin and the business of the fence. We made it into the headquarters ranch just a little before noon. We tied our horses near the bunkhouse and I said to Wilcey, "Ought to be about grub time. Let's eat."

We went to the cookhouse. It was plenty crowded. Didn't nobody say much of nothing to us so we just sat down and ate and didn't offer to be any too friendly ourselves. Well, it wasn't too hard to pick the hard cases out from the regular ranch hands. It looked to me like they'd hired every gunhand in about six counties.

But, then, I reckoned me and Wilcey looked about the same. We were all sitting at that one long table, maybe forty of us or so, and you could see the fence riders grouped off from the regular working hands.

Me and Wilcey just kept our horns in, not saying anything to anybody. I didn't see Sawyer or Gaines or anybody I knew. But when the meal was over I did ask one old boy when they were paying off.

"Right at one o'clock," he said. "Right out at that

table under the big oak in front of the ranch house. The major himself."

Well, I didn't know who the fuck the major was and didn't much give a damn. All I wanted to do was collect what little money we had coming and get into town and have us a little good times.

We went outside and went around to the front of the ranch headquarters and found us the sunniest spot we could and just sat there sucking on matches and smoking and waiting for payday.

They had a table set out under a big oak tree in the front. I reckoned that was probably the only tree in thirty miles and how it came to get as big as it did was anybody's guess.

But, after a time, Bob Danning came out and set himself up a chair and laid a whole bunch of papers down on the table. Then Ormsby come out and kind of looked around and then went on back in. After that Gaines come out. Ormsby hadn't noticed us, but Gaines damn sure did. But he just looked at us, making no sign.

After that the whole bunch of them went on back in the headquarters house. Most of the hands were beginning to gather up, just kind of squatting around, waiting for the money to come forth.

I was smoking a cigarillo and I told Wilcey, "I swear, if I ever get myself in such a fix again I hope somebody blows a hole through me. I can't believe I'm settin' around here waitin' for some sonofabitch to come give me a hundred dollars."

"Fifty," he said.

"What?"

"It's fifty, not a hundred. Remember, we already drawed an advance on our wages."

"Oh, yeah," I said sourly. "I forgot. I just thought I was low when I was standing around like a little puppy dog waiting for a hundred. Now I find out I'm about half again as low as that."

Well, after we all got pretty well gathered up, out came the whole procession. There was Ormsby and Danning and Gaines and Sawyer and a couple of hands I'd never seen carrying a chest. Last of all came a little pouter pigeon of a man wearing a suit and carrying a cane and smoking a cigar. By now there were enough ranch hands around so I could nudge one and ask, "Who the hell is that?"

"That's the major," he said. "He's the one runs the bunch that owns this outfit. He's the big owner."

Well, that kind of got my curiosity up and I commenced to ask around a little more about the major. Came to find out he'd been a major in the Yankee army, which was where he got his title, and he was the head nigger in a Chicago syndicate that owned the Skillet.

I told Wilcey, "I didn't like this operation at first and now I like it even less."

Well, after a little time they got set up to pay off. Danning and Ormsby set down at the table. Ormsby had the papers in front of him and Danning had a whole raft of gold coins up in front of him. Sawyer and Gaines were standing behind both of them with rifles. I reckoned they figured somebody was going to try and rob them.

But I'll tell you, my eyes were kind of taken by the amount of that gold coin they had on the table. It plenty surprised me. I took it to be at least $10,000.

I said to Wilcey, "Would you look at that."

"That's a bunch," he said.

Well, they finally started paying off. The way they did it was we all got in line like a bunch of goddamn sheep and passed by the table. You came up there and Danning asked you if you was so and so and you said, "Yes"—some of the hands even said, "Yes, sir,"—and then Danning said you had so much coming and then you took another step and Ormsby counted out your money.

And all this while that little pouter pigeon of a major was standing around smoking his cigar and leaning on his cane. I reckon he was waiting for some of us to come up and kiss his boots for handing out the money.

When I went through the line there wasn't a real word said to me. Ormsby never even looked at me. I glanced at Gaines, standing behind him, but he just stood there, holding that rifle, and didn't give any sign.

Well, we got our money collected and then we cinched up and got on our horses and headed for town. On the way I remarked about that pile of gold coin they had. "Wonder how they got it out to the ranch?" I asked Wilcey. "They damn sure didn't grow it there."

"No idea," he said.

"The gold was in that chest them two hands lugged out."

"Reckon it was," he said.

I started to keep on wondering out loud, but then I thought, the hell with it. It was time to go on into town and have a little good times.

But, and make no mistake about this, I didn't like that ranch or its Yankee owners.

And, funny enough, I was already kind of missing Hester.

Well, we made it to Tascosa about mid-afternoon. The Tinhorn wasn't in his hotel room, but we slung our gear and bedrolls in there and then went looking for him in the most likely place, the biggest saloon in town.

Sure enough he was there, fixed up at a table and dealing stud to five ranch hands who ought to have had better sense than to have been trying to beat him at poker. He saw us come in, gave us a wink, finished out the hand, and then came over to where we'd set down at a table. The bartender had brought us a bottle and some glasses so we immediately poured out all around and knocked back a toast to luck.

We didn't say much of anything for a time. Finally Wilcey said, "I am goddamn glad to be out of that line-camp cabin."

The Tinhorn asked, "How's it been going?"

Wilcey gave him a sour look. "Well, Young here found himself a girl friend. But I'm still making out with stump-trained heifers."

I said, seriously, "I don't know how much more of that job we can take. How you been doing with the poker playing?"

He shrugged. "Still ahead, but not as good as it was. They starting to get a little leery of me."

Wilcey asked, "Them two whores still here you spoke about?"

"Oh, yes," the Tinhorn said. "I done warned them the two of you would be coming into town. I understand they are laying in for a long siege."

I wasn't doing much talking because I was thinking on something pretty heavy. So we just kind of sat there drinking, me and Wilcey cooling out from being fence riders and the Tinhorn just relaxing and waiting for us to rouse a little. Finally he did say something that caught my attention.

He said, "Well, I seen ya'll's payday taking off yesterday."

"What's that?"

"Oh, they took a bunch of gold out of the bank here and taken it out to that ranch ya'll work for. Looked like a small army guarding it. That one that hired ya'll and that Gaines fellow and two or three others. Loaded it in a little buckboard with one man driving and Ormsby riding on the seat with him and then the rest of them with rifles at the ready."

So that was where they got the gold. Out of the bank. "When did you say they done it?"

"Yesterday."

"Hmmmm," was all I said. I got up from the table and finished my drink. Then I said, "I'm gonna go out and walk around a spell. I got something I want to think about."

Wilcey said, "Want any company?"

I shook my head. "No. I got to figure this out for myself."

I was starting to feel a little twinge of excitement; I was starting to feel like I was about to be myself again.

For maybe an hour I walked around town, not even minding the cold wind, just thinking of all the possibilities. Then I went down to the train depot and rounded up the telegraph operator and sent Chula a telegram in care of his cousin in San Antonio.

That he got the telegram and could come to the Panhandle was vital because, in the way I was working it out, I would need him and need him bad. But, at that point, I had no idea where he was or what he was doing. All I knew was that I'd always been able to reach him through his cousin before and that if he wasn't dead or disabled he'd come as soon as he got the message.

After that I went back to the saloon. I was in a damned good mood and I guess it showed because the Tinhorn said, "Uh oh, Wilcey. He's done beat you to the ladies. That's where the sonofabitch has been. He wasn't out thinking. He was over at that hotel doing a little fucking."

But Wilcey just shook his head. "No, Young's got him a girl friend and you know him, he's a true-blue all the way."

Well, we drank for a while and then went over to the café and had us a good meal. After we'd had a cup of coffee, I said, "Let's go on back to the hotel."

Wilcey said, "Hell, it's early yet."

"Not to stay," I said. "I got something I want to talk to ya'll about and I want to do it in private."

Well, we went on up to the room and me and Wilcey sat on the beds while Preacher occupied the one chair. He had a bottle of whiskey and we got that out and took a pull and then I set the bottle down in the middle of the floor and said, "Well, I've figured out what we're going to do about our situation."

"What's that?" Wilcey asked me.

"We're going to rob the ranch's payroll."

They didn't either one say anything for a time and then Wilcey said, "Hell, Will, that's a kind of tall order. What makes you reckon we can pull off such a stunt?"

"I kind of got it figured out."

Wilcey said, "Where, out there at the ranch? My God, Will, they'd be fifty cowhands around. And if we try it the night before you know they got it locked in a safe and guarded. Hell, we couldn't get within a half mile of that money."

"Ain't thinking about the ranch," I said. "We'll have it before it gets to the ranch."

The Tinhorn said, "Out of the bank? Not likely! I know I damn sure don't want any part of that!"

I shook my head. "And not the bank either. On the road. On the road when they're taking it to the ranch."

The Tinhorn hooted and Wilcey said, "Didn't you hear Preacher tell you how well-guarded that money is? Hell, the three of us—and never mind how good you are—the three of us can't go up against them kind of guns."

"Yes, we can," I said steadily. "And it ain't going to be just the three of us. I think I got some help coming."

Well, naturally they wanted to know all about how I had it planned out, but I didn't want to talk about it. I didn't know all the details myself or how I was actually going to do it and it ain't too damn smart to talk about whether it's going to be a bull or a heifer before the cow drops the calf, so I just told them not to worry about it and that they'd know in plenty of time.

But it was worrying them both considerably. The Tinhorn said that he thought we had it pretty good and ought to continue like we were for the time being.

I answered him by saying, "Yes, that's all right for you, but you ain't where Wilcey and I are and it's a sight harder on us. No. We can't go on with the foolishness we are in."

Wilcey sided with me in that, but he did say, "Will, I'm considerably worried about this undertaking. I know you know a mile more about this robbing business than either one of us, but I'm damned if I can see how we can bring this off. Hell, to tell you the truth, I'm a little scared."

Well, we kept on talking and I finally got on to the subject of Chulo. Of course they were a good deal interested in him. Wilcey said, "Listen, I've heard you speak of the black Mexican a good number of times. Is he as mean as you say he is?"

I was smoking a cigarillo and I took a drag and then flipped it over against the wall. "Meaner," I said. "I ain't really done him justice in what I've told you."

"But, hell, we might have to go up against six men, six good men with guns. Me and Preacher can't handle that."

"No," I agreed, "but Chulo and I can."

"What makes you think he'll come?"

I just shook my head. "I don't think, I *know* he'll come if he gets my telegram."

"How you know he'll get your telegram?"

Again I shook my head. "I don't know. Hell, I ain't seen nor heard from the man in near three years. I'll just say this, if he don't come they ain't gonna be no robbery. How's that?"

Well, that sort of mollified them somewhat so we talked on a bit longer and then went out and did a little more drinking and then I went back to the hotel and went to bed while the Tinhorn commenced gambling and Wilcey ran down one of them whores and got his ashes hauled.

I heard them come in much later that night, but I was sleeping so good I didn't pay them any mind. They were both a little drunk and singing. But that was all right. A man is entitled to a little of that every once in a while.

We had us some good times for a couple of more days and then it came time for Wilcey and I to leave and go back to the line camp. The morning we were to ride out I told the Tinhorn, over breakfast, "Listen, if a mean-looking black Mexican comes around, don't get scared. I told him in the telegram to look you up and that you'd get him to me."

He said, "Shit, I been around you so long I ain't scared of nothing."

I also told them, "Now, don't start getting nervous about this job until I see we can pull it off. If it ain't this I'll think of something else."

And Wilcey said, "But god damnit, Will, this looks a little too rough. I wish you *would* think of something else."

I said, "It's the only money I see around here worth stealing. God damnit, what do you expect? I ain't gonna get you off in no storm."

We rode out of town heading back for the fence-riding job. Wilcey was down in the mouth worrying about the robbery, but I was in considerably better spirits than I'd been when I'd rode in. All I was worrying about was Chulo showing up.

For I knew I couldn't pull off the dangerous robbery I'd planned without his sure and steady gun hand.

We got back to that line-camp shack just before dark. We got the horses put up and then went on inside. Wilcey lit the lantern. Then he stood there shaking out the match for a minute. I was sitting on my bunk, just sitting there taking a drink out of a whiskey bottle. The lantern lighted up the shadows in the corners of the cabin. Wilcey went over and sat down on his bunk across from me. I pitched him the whiskey bottle and he took a drink.

Then he sat there looking at me with me looking at him. The coldness of the damn shack was coming down on both of us. He took a slow look around, seeing where we was.

I knew he was scared about the robbery.

He asked me, "Will, you reckon we can really do it?"

I said, "Yeah, I reckon so, Wilcey." He'd pitched me back the bottle and I said, "That or get kilt in the attempt."

He said, in the dry voice of his, "That's what worries me."

I just asked him, "Well, what would you druther?"

He took a slow look around the cabin, listening, I'd imagined, to the wind whistling through them cracks. Then he picked up the bottle and took a drink. "Hell," he finally said, "why not?"

I give it a minute or two longer and then I asked him, "Wilcey, you really want to do this? I tell you, I'm wanted all over the state, but you ain't. And this job will get you in the shape I'm in. You might ought to think about it."

He sat there studying the cigarillo he'd lit, thinking

about it. Finally he asked me, "Will, you reckon we'll all get killed on this?"

I let it lay long enough to give credit to the kind of serious question it was. But I could no more have answered it knowing than if he'd have given me ten thousand years to have come up to the question. You don't go into a killing situation with any guarantees you ain't going to be the one who gets killed.

I just finally said, "Wilcey, I hope not."

"You think we can bring it off?"

I said, "Oh, Wilcey, quit playing the calf. How the hell do I know? We're going to try."

"Then tell me about this Chulo. You seem to be putting a lot of stock in him. Tell me about him."

Well, I thought about it a long moment. I wanted to try and tell him about Chulo as exact as I could. Finally I took my revolver out of the holster and showed it to him. I said, "You remember when I got cabin fever so bad last month that I damn near shot you?"

He kind of half nodded and I said, "Well, Chulo *would have* shot you."

He didn't say anything and I said, "Let me explain it better. That's the meanest one-eyed black goddamn Mexican that ever lived and I'd rather have him on my side than a troop of U.S. cavalry. Is that straight?"

He kind of looked at me for a moment, but then he didn't say anything else. He just kind of went to bed and I did the same. We lay there a half hour and then I could hear him rustling around. He asked me, "Will, you reckon we can do it?"

I said, "Hell no. I'm just guessing at it. Now, go to sleep and shut your face."

Well, we didn't talk about it much the next day, just kind of fell back into the style we'd been in; ride that goddamn fence and eat in between times. Drink a little whiskey and play a little nickel poker. I tell you, I

WILSON'S CHOICE 113

figured it was going to be the longest month of my life.

And I reckoned it was worse on Wilcey because he didn't have him a Hester to visit every three or four nights.

But then it wasn't awful easy on me because Hester was beginning to get kind of under my skin. Hell, she acted exactly like the kind of woman I needed. But I knew there was nowhere for us to go, not with me fixing to rob the goddamn payroll off that ranch. I didn't have a safe place I could take her, not as wanted as I was, even if she'd been willing to leave her dead husband's ranch and go with me.

We sat one night at her eating table, not saying much of anything to each other. I wanted to tell her about the robbery we were planning, but I knew that would be the end of us. She wasn't so dumb that she wouldn't be able to figure out that as soon as I done that deed I'd have to get out of the country. And I didn't want to spoil the little pleasure I had going until I just had to.

Oh, I tell you, she was a man-pleasing, sweet-loving woman. And it seemed that since I'd come she'd just literally commenced to blossom. She never knew when I was going to show up, but she was always dressed and prettied up as much as she could be with the little she had to help herself with.

Well, we sat there, me plenty contented after a good dinner and a few drinks of whiskey in my belly. I wanted to take her to bed, but I didn't feel right about it. I could tell she was starting to care for me, as I was for her, and I knew she'd already been hurt pretty bad one time and that I ought not to hurt her again.

I was trying to think of something to say when she suddenly spoke up. She said, almost as if she were talking to somebody else, "I reckon a man could make a living on this little piece of ground my husband left me. That is if he was a mind to quit robbing and killing. Seems like he'd be far enough from the law out here that they wouldn't think to look for him. That is if he was ready to quit all his meanness and not bring none down on his head around here."

Well, there wasn't much I could say to that, even if I'd known what to say. All I knew was that the wind was whistling around the corners and it was cold outside, but it was mighty warm sitting in that cabin with that good woman. I finally said, "Com'on, let's go to bed."

She said, "But it be early yet. I ain't sleepy."

"We ain't going to bed to sleep."

"Oh," was all she said. She got up immediately and began getting ready.

Later on that night I was sitting up at the table smoking a cigarillo and having a last drink of whiskey before going to sleep. She was laying on her back with her eyes closed and I figured she was already asleep. I had the lamp wick trimmed down low and it was so dim in the cabin that I couldn't see her face. But her voice suddenly came out of the dark. She said, "What's going to become of us?"

I said, "What?"

"What's going to become of us? What's to happen?"

"To who?"

"To us. To you and I."

Well, I kind of knew what she meant, but I didn't want to reply to that kind of question. So I said, "Hell, we'll go on. Just like everybody else."

She was a long time in saying anything and then she just said, "All right." I could hear the disappointment in her voice. It made me feel bad. But I didn't know what else to say. Hell, I didn't have no future to promise her. Finally I just finished my whiskey, put out the lantern, and went to bed. She didn't make any move to get nearer to me after I got in bed, as had been her habit.

Of course visiting Hester I was neglecting my duties and I knew that sooner or later it would show up. As it did the next day as I was going from her shack down the fence to our line camp. In about the same place as before about fifty yards of fence had been taken down. I figured it was the same old man and his sons. They were either hazing more cattle north or else they were bringing back the ones they'd already taken in. But it was getting on toward afternoon and I didn't want to stick around and take the chance of getting caught out at night with the weather looking bad so I just fixed the fence and rode on to our shack.

Wilcey wasn't back yet so I turned my horse in and got me a drink of whiskey and water and got a fire going. The weather had abated some, but they still wasn't anybody going to mistake the place for the sunny climes of the border country.

He sat down on his bunk opposite me and took a straight drink out of the bottle of whiskey. He looked tired.

"Ought to put a little water with that," I said.

He just shook his head. "Boy, I'm getting tired of this goddamn life. I wish we was pulling that robbery tomorrow."

"I thought you was a little nervous about it."

"Hell, I am. But this goddamn foolishness we're doing right now is going to slowly drive me crazy. Ride all day over that same ground. In all that cold. Shit! Come back here and live like a nigger in this shack. Anything's got to be better than this."

So you could see how bad it was getting if it was bothering the generally mild and even-tempered Wilcey.

But we got some unexpected good news that night. Not very long after dark the door suddenly opened and in walked the Tinhorn. And be goddamned if he didn't have a telegram for me. I'd had him checking the telegraph office every day and the one he was holding had come in right after noon. So the Tinhorn had jumped on his horse and lit a shuck for our cabin.

"What's it say?" Wilcey asked me.

I tore the envelope open and scanned the few words. "Says he's coming," I said. "Damn good."

"When?" Wilcey wanted to know.

I shrugged. "Soon's he can. Soon's he can get up here. I would reckon he's already got his horse pointed north. He'll be here in plenty of time."

"I bet he don't."

"Yes, he will," I insisted. "He's a good man."

"He don't know when the robbery is."

"No, that's true. But he's already started from the way his telegram reads. And it's only about five hundred miles and he can ship his horse and himself part of the way on the train. Stop worrying. You're fighting your head."

The Preacher asked, "What's the matter?"

"Oh," I said, "your partner is getting himself a little case of the jitters, mixed in with about a half a bucketful of cabin fever and a gallon of woman-wishing."

"What's woman-wishing?"

"That's wishing you had a woman when you ain't, can't, and won't get one."

So we settled down for the long wait. The unfortunate part of it was there was really no planning to the robbery. We were just fixing to get into the roadagent business. It was as simple as that. We couldn't rob them at the ranch; there were too many hands around who would think we were stealing their money. They'd have it locked in a vault at the bank.

Therefore, the only logical place to take them was on the road between the bank and the ranch. Of course they'd be well armed, but I didn't think they'd be as ready as they ought to because they wouldn't think there was anybody in that country crazy enough to stick them up.

The only one of the guards, or at least of the men the Tinhorn said he'd seen guarding the gold, that I was worried about was Gaines. But then I'd have Chulo to help me with him. Wilcey would be a big help on the job and the Tinhorn would be all right because I was going to put a gun in his hand, but I was going to be sure he wouldn't be in a position to get hurt or mess the job up.

So that's what I meant about not having much planning to do. All we'd do would be to jump them somewhere on the road and say, "Stick 'em up!" After that it would be decided by if they wanted to fight or not and, if so, how the fight went.

But the waiting was made unexpectedly difficult by something that crept in my mind a couple of days after I was back from Hester's the last time. I was lying in bed staring up at the dark ceiling and, all of a sudden I got to thinking about what Hester had said, about a man could make a living on that little piece of ground her dead husband had left and wouldn't have to be worried about the law in that remote piece of the country.

That is if he kept himself straight on his home range.

Well, that was probably true, but the question was, what kind of living could he make and was I, in spite of all my big talk, really desirous of settling down to a work-a-day life and grubbing out a living off a few head of cattle and whatever else could be raised on a poor place.

Still, it would be the settled life and there would be

the woman to make up for a lot of stiffness in a man's bones after he'd done a hard day's work in the cold and snow or in the blistering heat.

It kind of startled me, thinking about it, for if I'd really meant what I said about leaving the owl-hoot trail, here was the chance to do it, and I wouldn't need no big stake either. It wouldn't be the horse ranch I'd dreamed of, but it would be the good wife and some land, however little and however poor, and it would provide a living, for witness the fact that a woman was making out single-handedly on the place.

And I wouldn't be running and dodging and fearing for my capture or death at every moment. And I wouldn't be an outlaw anymore with every man's hand against me.

But what would I do about Wilcey and the Tinhorn?

Well, hell, they'd been making out before they met me and would probably be doing a damn sight better if they'd *never* met me.

Lying there in the dark I toyed with the idea of not doing the robbery, just saying to my partners that I'd decided to marry Hester and settle down and give up the outlaw game.

Well, it was something to think of, but it was too much for me that night so I just finally gave it up and went to sleep.

But it was still on my mind the next day when I rode out to take the ten-mile patrol that day. The one thing I was hoping was that we could somehow avoid a shooting, or any kind of trouble for that matter, about that goddamn fence until we could get that robbery pulled off. Wilcey and I had talked it over the night before. He asked me what I thought he ought to do if he ran on to someone crossing the fence. I'd shrugged and said I didn't know. "Don't do nothing."

"Yeah, but if we get caught doing nothing we'll get fired and then we ain't going to have no reason to be around this country when it comes time to pull the robbery."

Well, he had a point there. In fact I was just thinking on that, that and Hester, when I had the misfortune to come across that old man and his two idiot-looking sons in the very act of cutting that fence so they could let their sorry-looking cattle back south. It was a clear, cold day, and I could see their breath steaming in the air. "God damnit!" I swore. I put my horse into a hard run, bearing down on them. "Hold it! Hold it! God damnit! Hold it!" I was yelling as I charged them, jerking out my saddle gun as I did. I come charging up, skidding my horse to a stop. They just stood there, all of them afoot with wire cutters in their hands, looking up at me with those same simple, give-out expressions on their faces.

I said, "Now, god damnit, old man, you got to quit this! You know I can't let you take that fence down." I sat my horse, his sides heaving between my legs, my rifle lying across the pommel. The old man just stared back at me.

"I got to move these cattle south, mister. And ain't no way you can stop me."

God damnit, that irritated me. I said, "I can shoot you, you old bastard."

But he just shook his head at that. "It's all one," he said, "shoot us or starve us out. We daid either way. And shootin's faster."

"Aw, shit," I said. I didn't know what to do. Listen, we were pretty low on supplies and the supply wagon was due along at any time. There was nothing to keep the supply wagon driver from topping a rise and taking word back to the company headquarters that we weren't doing our job.

Or one of them other riders from one of the other

line camps. They could see me lettin' a bunch of nestors through the fence and not raising my hand to stop them.

I said, "Listen, you are going to get me in trouble."

"Kain't be hep'ed," he said, and reached over and cut a strand of wire with his pinchers. Then he walked on down to the next post and jerked the wire loose from the staple so that it came off in a long line. They'd already taken down the top strand and now he was commencing to handle the middle one. Swearing, I got off my horse and walked over and, shoving him in the chest with the barrel of my rifle, pushed him back from the fence.

"Now, get away from there," I said. "And move along."

"Kain't," he said. "Got to get these cattle south and this here fence is in the way." He made a move toward the fence and I shoved him back again.

"Don't do that," I said. But it didn't seem to do any good to threaten him; he didn't seem to care. Behind me I heard a snip and looked back and one of his boys was cutting the wire behind me.

"Aw, hell!" I said in disgust. The only way I could stop them would be to shoot them and I didn't much think that was my style. I looked both ways up and down the fence and didn't see anybody coming. "All right," I said in disgust. I went and mounted my horse. "Get your sorry-ass cattle through the fence, but make sure it's the last time. And I mean it! Next time I shoot you."

He didn't say anything. I started to ride off and then stopped right by him. "And put that goddamn fence back up when you get your cattle through."

He still didn't answer, just went on working with his pinchers. "I said put that fence back up when you're passed."

Then he did look up at me. He said, "Mister, I kin

guarantee you I ain't never gonna put strand one of this here fence back up!"

That did make me angry. I said, "Old man, what is your name?"

"Sutter," he said. "An' I ain't nevah been ashamed of it!"

"All right, Sutter," I said, "where is your place? Where do you live?"

He pointed south. "About six miles yonder."

"Then get this straight. I ever find this fence cut again I'm coming to find you and make no mistake."

"Best brang some grub with ye. We got little enough for ourselves. Much less for feedin' com'ny."

"Aw, shit!" I said. I put spurs to my horse and started on up the fence line. I looked back after a half mile and Sutter and his boys were up on their sorry-ass cow-hocked horses, driving their worthless hides through the gap. Pretty soon I started laughing. If everybody in the world wasn't any more scared of my guns than old man Sutter, I'd have been out of work.

I told Wilcey about it that night and we had a pretty good laugh.

He said, "Shit, I'm glad I haven't run into him. I don't know what I'd of done. He'd of probably had me helping him tear that fence down."

Wilcey had been lucky so far; he hadn't run into anyone on his patrols.

The supply wagon come in not long after that and the driver stayed the night with us since it was already late. He was a long, tall, drink of water who'd been at the ranch some twenty years. He was a pretty good old boy, though not too long on the smarts. I talked him out for a few extra supplies, with an eye to leaving Hester as well off as I could when we pulled stakes.

He said some of the camps on the eastern end had been having a pretty lively time of it.

He was sitting on my bunk eating a plate of beans, his Adam's apple going up and down in his scrawny neck every time he swallowed.

"Yeah," he said, "bunch of rustlers or some such got after a stretch of fence right before the last camp and them two guards got into it pretty hot with 'em." His eyes got big. "One of them guards got shot! Shot in the shoulder! I know 'cause I's the one carried him to headquarters for doctorin'!"

He said the camps nearer to headquarters hadn't been having much trouble. "Boss is talkin' 'bout reinforcin' them fer camps. Heered some talk 'bout it might be you two gits sent up thar to h'ep. Wouldn't that be somethin'!"

He seemed to think it would be a compliment to our gun skills or what not, but it just gave Wilcey and me a sinking feeling. The far camp was at least 150 miles from where we wanted to pull off the robbery.

I asked the driver if he'd heard anything else, but he just shook his head. "Naw, other'n they's a power of folks on these here plains jest flat don't cotton to that fence. But they might's well hush they bellyachin'. Mister Ormsby and the major be a mind to see that fence stay. So I reckon she'll stay."

After a time he spread his bedroll on the floor and went straight to sleep, but what he'd said left Wilcey and I considerably troubled. We walked out in the cold night to look at the horses and I told Wilcey, "If they order us up there the only thing we can do is quit. We'd never be back here at the right time to pull off that robbery. Not with Chulo and the Tinhorn in town. We got to be able to stay in steady communication."

He agreed and we went in and went to bed, but didn't go to sleep right off.

So we went on with the waiting. I was going to Hester's more and more. She was considerably on my mind and what she'd said was considerably on my mind. I took her some more supplies. She didn't want to take them, but she did because she had to. She didn't mention anymore about what she'd said, about an outlaw settling down and ranching her little place, but she did say, kind of looking away from me when she said it, "Lord, Will, I still can't believe ye came along when ye did. I was near at the end of my rope and I don't know what I'd of done iffen it hadn't of been for you. If you was to go tomorrow and ne'er come back I'd still be allus grateful to ye."

It stayed pretty good between us though, as I say, I was much troubled as to what to do about her. One night I was sitting at the table, eating supper and she, as was still her custom, was standing behind me seeing to my wants. I all of a sudden asked her, "Hester, what would you say if two days before the end of the month I was to tell you to hitch up your buggy and head for Amarillo? Would you go?"

"What are you saying, sir?" She came and poured me some more coffee and, without my asking, added a little whiskey to it from the bottle I kept sitting on the table. "My lands, that's the strangest question I ever heard a body ask. Why in the world would you want me to go to Amarillo? And why just so, just the two days before the end of the month. Lands, I don't even know what day it is."

I passed on that and said, "And I mean alone. Without me. But with good prospects I'd be joining you there."

She came around the table in front of me and gave me a perplexed look. "What ever in the world are you talking about, sir?"

I was a good long moment answering her because I be go to hell if I knew what I was saying either. I took a drink of the coffee and whiskey and then a bite of the beefsteak she'd fried up for me and sat there chewing and thinking. Even if she could get to Amarillo on her own, and even if she could get on a train and find her way to some destination I'd picked on the border, and even if I did make it there by a separate route, I really had nothing to offer her except a life on the dodge. No, it was an idea like Todd, my old partner, might have had. It was foolish.

But I said, "It's a long forty miles down there and a woman in a buggy would take two days to do it. That'd put you out there on that prairie at least one night by yourself. No, that'd be too risky."

Which kind of got her dander up, though I hadn't intended it to. She said, "I beg yore pardon, sir. If I was a mind to get myself to Amarillo in two days by myself I reckon I could do it." She had a little heat in her voice. "I managed to survive out here on this ranch with no help from nobody for a good many months before you came along. So don't you be telling me what I can manage."

I looked up at her. "Well, would you do it?"

She stood there, holding the coffee pot, regarding me. "For what reason, sir?"

I shook my head. "I can't tell you that."

"Then, sir, in a word, no!"

But after a while, while we were sitting in front of the fire staring into the flames, she said, "But what would I do with my stock?"

I shrugged. "Get old man Sutter to look after it."

She gave a start. "What do you know of Mister Sutter?"

I grimaced. "More than I want to." Then I told her what had happened.

It brought a smile to her face, an expression I rarely saw. "Oh, yes," she said, "that sounds like Mister Sutter."

"Or give them to him," I said.

"Oh, I couldn't do that!"

"Why not?"

"Why, it's my living. I couldn't give away my living."

"Your living? Hell, maybe you don't understand. You meet me in Amarillo and your living is going to be me."

I guess she really hadn't understood before because my saying it like that really caught her up short. She finally said, kind of stammering, "What—what are you saying, sir?"

"I'm saying that if you come to Amarillo and then do as I tell you, I will be your living."

She said, "Does that—" She stopped. "I mean, does that—Are you saying that—"

She stopped and I said, "It means nothing. Look, let's forget it for the night and go to bed. I'm tired."

But I lay there that night thinking I'd let my mouth overload my ass again. Hell, I could barely take care of myself. How the hell did I propose to take care of a wife? Especially a wife that knew less of the world than any woman I'd ever known. She was no Cata, the sister of a receiver of stolen cattle; she was no Linda, half whore, half hustler; she was different from any woman I'd ever met before.

But could I ride off and leave her on this godforsaken prairie to rot? Or take her off on the dodge with me and end up getting her killed?

Hell, I didn't know what to do. And that was becoming a way of life for me.

When we got up the next morning I was afraid she was going to bring it up. But she didn't, just fixed my breakfast and took care of my needs as nice as a man could want. I went out and saddled my horse and fed her stock and, when I came back to the shack, she was waiting with my noon meal all fixed and packed for me. I kissed her, told her I'd see her in a few days, then mounted and rode off.

* * *

One night, just after we'd come in, me and Wilcey were sitting there arguing about who was going to fix supper and having a drink of whiskey. About then the door opened and in walked the Tinhorn and, right behind him was Chulo. I looked up, seeing his black, swarthy, ugly, mean face. I just shook my head. "Oh, shit!" I said. I turned to Wilcey, "Hide the women and the whiskey, the goddamn black Mexican is here."

"Halo, *amigo*!" he said. He came over and I got up and we gave each other a big *abrazo*, which is the custom among Mexican men, to hug each other and pound each other on the back.

We immediately got us out some more cups and poured out all around, straight whiskey this time, then knocked them back as befits the toast.

"Luck," me and Wilcey and the Tinhorn said.

"*Buena suerte*," Chulo said.

Well, I was that glad to see him, and he looked as mean as ever. He'd gotten himself a black patch for that eye he'd lost on the job we'd pulled when we held up that train. Seeing it reminded me of how he'd borne up to the pain of the thing during the week we'd had to hide out after the job. The way his face had swole up and the fluid and stuff that had run out of his eye—you knew it was damn near killing him, but he'd never let on, other than to bust out cussing ever' once in a while and to drink a little more whiskey than usual.

Of course it was hard to tell when he was drinking more whiskey than usual.

He didn't look none too prosperous, more like he might have come on some hard times himself. But he was still carrying that big Navy Colt revolver at his side and he was still wearing a pair of them silver-mounted big-rowled Mexican spurs that jingled every time he moved his leg. And he was still wearing that black flat-crowned hat like he'd always done. Though up in the cold he had it tied on his head with a scarf just like the rest of us.

He'd found us just as I'd predicted; shipped himself and his horse to Amarillo, which was the nearest railhead from us, then came on to Tascosa and looked up the Tinhorn as I'd told him to do in my telegram. After that they'd mounted up and come a-calling.

After a time we got kind of settled and sort of sat back and talked. He asked me, "Say, Weelson, how com' you pick such a goddamn cold place to make a leetle money, heh?"

"Shit," I said, "they done shipped it all north. We had to come up here to get it."

I'd known Chulo a good long time and, though we'd never rode together on a regular thing, we'd been on a few jobs together, the railroad holdup being by far the biggest. But he was a damn good man, and no mistake.

I'd talked about him enough that I didn't really have to fill my partners in over much.

But I wanted to know what had happened to him since we'd robbed that train. It had been damn near three years. "Well, *amigo*," I said, "what the hell you been doing with yourself? Been making any money?"

"A leetle," he said.

"Doing what? Or I mean, robbing who?"

He grinned, his white teeth showing big in his black face. "A leetle this, *un poquito eso*." He lit a cigarillo. "Mostly I rob the Mexican cattle and sell them to my leetle cousin in San Antonio. He is a good man to sell cattle to." He laughed.

Which kind of surprised me. Hell, he and I had gotten away with near $14,000 in gold off that train robbery. I knew what had happened to mine, but I couldn't figure his. I asked him and he laughed again and held up one finger.

"For one year Chulo is one big man. Spend plenty money on wheeskey and the ladies and the *comida*. Plenty big man." He laughed again and shrugged. "Pretty soon the money is gone and Chulo ain't such a beeg man no more. So I go back and steal the cattle for my cousin."

Well, that wasn't too hard to figure. I'd been doing the same for a good many more years than I wanted to think about. Finally Chulo turned to me kind of casual and asked, "*Qué paso, amigo?*"

Or, what kind of job have you got lined up?

Well, I laid it out for him as best I could. At first, when I'd telegraphed him, I'd been worried that he wouldn't think the job would be big enough—ten thousand split between four men. After all, in the last robbery we'd been on together there'd been considerably more. But, as down at the heels as he was, he wasn't much better off than the four of us and $2500 ought to look pretty good.

I quitted by saying, "Well, that's about it. It's a holdup on the road out on the bald-ass prairie and then a hell of a run to the border. They might not be any shooting, but my guess is there will be. If they is it will mainly fall on you and I. Wilcey is good, but not a gunman. Neither is the Preacher. They'll have one good *pistolero*. His name is Gaines. If we get the chance the Preacher will point him out to you in town. If he comes in like I hear he does. But you just stay the hell away from him. I don't want them connecting up what you're doing in town to that gold being moved out to that ranch. In fact, I don't want them seeing you and the Preacher together. You just hang around town and keep your horns pulled in. That is if you go in with us. Now, how does it sound?"

I sat back and waited for his answer. He just shrugged. "*Cómo no?*"

"Then you're in?"

WILSON'S CHOICE 129

"*Sequera*," he said. "You still *loco*, Weelson. You then' I come thes far to say no?"

Well, that made us all feel pretty damn good. We poured out all around and then knocked them straight back again for luck. I already began to feel like I was going to get out of that goddamn place. And with a piece of that goddamn ranch's money.

I asked Chulo how his eye was. He touched the patch and shrugged.

"*No importa*," he said. "It is only my left eye. I shoot with my right hand and my right eye."

We laughed and I held up one finger like we used to do. I tried to imitate the way he talked. "I like to robe one Texican ranchero."

"*Cómo no?*" he said. Why not?

He and I pitched our bedrolls on the floor while Wilcey and the Preacher took the bunks. Chulo and I sat on the floor after the others had gone to bed, keeping the fire glowing and drinking whiskey and talking. We had a lot of *años* and territory to cover in the years since we'd seen each other. Finally I asked him how Cata was.

"She is married," he said. "She grieved bad after you left, but, pretty soon, an *hombre* comes from Mexico who don't know she'd been married to that *bandito* that got killed and so she married him and goes to live in Mexico. She is good now, I theenk."

Well, I was glad to hear it. In her own way Cata had been a good woman. Maybe the second best I'd known.

Chapter Five

Chulo and the Tinhorn rode back into Tascosa the next morning. It was clear he couldn't stay at the line camp, for the chance of discovery by another fence rider or by a checkup from the home ranch was too likely and we couldn't afford for him to be seen with us. They rode away after we had another drink to luck and some breakfast. I'd given the Tinhorn strict instructions to find out anything else he could about the transportation of the gold, but to be damned careful how he asked.

When they were gone me and Wilcey went back in the shack and commenced to get ready for the day's ride. I had the five-mile patrol that day so he'd be leaving before I would. We were both considerably cheered by Chulo having shown up.

Wilcey said, "Yeah. I feel like we can do it now. What the hell's the date? How much longer now?"

It was the twenty-fourth of January. We had seven days still to go to the thirty-first when we calculated they'd be moving the gold in order to pay off the men on the first.

Well, he got off on his patrol and I hunted me up a piece of brown wrapping paper, then found me a stub of a pencil, got me a cup of coffee and whiskey, then sat down at this little table we'd made out of some crates and some wood that was left over from building the shack.

I was going to draw me a map to kind of get my bearings and kind of lay the whole thing out in my mind. First I drew me a line across the paper from left to right. That was the fence. Then I spotted in the town of Tascosa over to the left or the west side of the paper about four miles south of the fence. It seemed like the ranch was about six miles north and a little to the east of the town so I spotted it in about two miles north of the fence, connecting them up with a wavy line to represent the little road that ran out that way. The Canadian River was about a mile, mile and a half out of town. The road crossed it at a little shallow ford. I drew that in, kind of shivering it a little to show it was water. The river was important in my plan. Where the road crossed it was about the only cover on that bald-ass prairie where road agents could hide and wait for their victims. Of course the cover was none too good; just a few medium-sized rocks and some bare willows and what looked to be scrub oaks growing along its banks. But if it was the only cover, then it was going to have to do.

After that I drew an X for our line camp, placing it what I reckoned was twenty miles east of the main headquarters and right on the fence line. Then I made another X for Hester's place. I placed her on a line about as far from the fence as Tascosa and a little more to the west than our camp. Then, based on what Sutter had told me and what Hester had told me, I put in a double XX for the old man's shack. I put him about two miles south of the town and about as far east as our line camp.

Then I got up and got me some more coffee and whiskey and lit a cigarillo and sat back to study my handiwork.

I sat there, puffing on my cigarillo, studying on it. Well, there was only one way. And that was to hit them at the river crossing, hit them right after they got across. But, Lord, it was going to be hard to conceal four horsemen right there by the edge of the road. They'd see us halfway across the river just as sure as shooting. Well, the only thing we could do then was to pick them off as fast as possible and hope we could stop them before they got back to town if they turned and ran.

But I was going to think on it some more and see if I could come up with a better idea.

There was one other thing I was going to have to change. I'd been thinking of taking our own horses, mine and Chulo's and Wilcey's and the Tinhorn's, out to Hester's the day before the robbery and leaving them and using the string of ranch horses to pull the job. That way we'd take off from the robbery heading east and a little to the north and that might give them the idea we were making for the Oklahoma territory. But it would also give us fresh horses after we'd made a hard run to get away. We would stop at Hester's, throw our saddles on our better-grade, well-rested horses, turn the ranch horses loose, and then head straight south for the border.

But now I wasn't sure about that, wasn't sure about it at all. Without thinking on it much I'd resolved, sometime, in my mind to talk Hester into leaving that sorry piece of land and going with me. If she did she'd be leaving early and we couldn't leave our horses there with no one to look after them for two days. And, besides that, even if she wouldn't go with me, I didn't really want to take the chance of involving her in this robbery in any shape, form, or fashion.

So I sat there and looked at Sutter's place. If anything it would be handier than Hester's. And closer. We could make a feint to the northeast for a mile or so or until we got out of sight over the horizon, and then turn and make a straight dash south for Sutter's. When we got to his place we'd actually be below Tascosa and not much more than thirty-five miles from Amarillo.

That is if we went to Amarillo. And the only reason we'd be going anywhere near there was if Hester were to meet me there. Other than that we'd stick to the open country.

I eyed it, thinking. With fresh horses at Sutter's, especially horses that befit men in our line of work, we could make that thirty-five miles in a day.

Well, it was another thing I probably ought to chew over in my mind.

I finally hid the map in amongst our food goods and went out and got my horse and set off about my patrol. I had told Wilcey if he ever ran into the old man Sutter just to not kill him or run him off.

I set out on my patrol with anxiety in my heart. I figured it would be just my luck, close as we were getting to our goal and as likely as it was beginning to get, that one of us would get into some kind of scrape about the goddamn fence and all our plans would go a-glimmering.

But I comforted myself that day with the thought that the next day it would be my turn for the long patrol and I could go and see Hester. There were very few times left now to see her. A couple of days before the holdup Chulo and the Tinhorn would be coming to the camp and it would be dangerous for me to absent myself. Besides, if all went as planned, she would be leaving then. There were six days to go. At most I could see her twice more.

That night I debated telling Wilcey what I was planning about Hester, but at the last moment decided not to. There was no need before it was a sure thing and, even so, it would just have worried him. His opinion of women and his opinion of my luck with women were none too good. He'd become convinced immediately that it would bitch the job. Well, it could have a bearing on my partners. I intended, after this job, that we should all go to the border and set up shop in Mexico. But I didn't know about that. If I took Hester with me I wasn't sure I could do that.

Oh, Lord, I tell you I was torn and no mistake. Hell, I was going to be wrong either way I went.

That next night I decided, while we were eating supper, I was going to tell her straight out what I had in mind and see what she wanted to do. I was already beginning to kind of tense up about the job and, I tell you straight, the woman was putting a burden on me she didn't even realize.

But, then, women never realize these things.

I said, "Hester, you going to meet me in Amarillo?"

"My, sir, what kind of talk is that? Whatever do you mean?"

She was standing there like she always was and I reached up and grabbed her arm and forced her in a chair. "Now, god damnit," I said, "sit down here and talk to me. This is serious. And I'll have no more of your playacting!"

Well, it got her attention. Her face got kind of white and she sat there looking a little more startled than I'd ever seen her.

"Now I ast you a question. And I want an answer."

She looked like a little girl. She said, in a kind of plaintive voice, "But I don't know what you mean?"

"I asked you if you'd leave here two days before the end of the month so as to make Amarillo by the time I get there. That's only about four or five days away."

I didn't want her telling me again that she didn't know what calendar day it was.

She looked at me, knowing I was serious, but still not knowing what I meant. Not knowing how to reply and afraid to make the wrong reply. Finally she said, "If you could just explain a little more."

I said, "I'm quitting this range then."

"Oh!" It made her draw her breath in. "Oh, dear."

I sat and looked at her. Hell, to tell you the truth I was boiling mad and didn't know why. I guess I was angry because she was complicating my life and I didn't much like that.

Finally she said, "So you be leaving."

"Ain't that what I just said?"

It kind of scared her, the tone of my voice. She said, "But I don't understand. If you be going, why do I have to go to Amarillo by myself? Why can't I go with you?"

I got up then from the table, kind of trying to walk my anger off. I walked over in the corner and threw the butt of my cigarillo down; then I walked back to the table and took a strong slug of whiskey; then I went over and stared at the fire a minute. I knew I oughtn't to tell her what I was fixing to tell her and I knew I was jeopardizing my partners, but the goddamn woman was making me so damn mad.

Complicating my life as she was.

I sat down at the table. "Listen," I asked her, "what the hell did I tell you I was? What I did for a living?"

"Well—" she said. "Weeelll—"

"God damnit!" I hit the table with my fist. It made her jump.

"You—you saaaid—" She kind of gulped. "You said—"

"What did I say I was?"

"You said—" Her voice was trembling, but she took a deep breath and said, "You said you was a well-wanted outlaw and killer." Then she kind of looked afraid, like I was fixing to hit her.

I sat back in my chair. "All right. And that's what I am. And that's why you have to meet me in Amarillo by yourself."

"I don't understand," she said.

I leaned toward her. "Woman, you don't seem to understand anything. I told you I'm quitting this range. Now, do you want to go with me or not?"

She looked hesitant and wouldn't answer.

Finally she kind of whispered, "As your wife?"

"That'll come later," I said. I knew that question had been on her lips for some time. "But the way we'll be traveling we might not be able to stop off and visit with a preacher for some little time. But if them goddamn words they say over you is so all-fired important, I'll do it at the first chance."

"Well," she said. "Well, I don't know what to say."

"I'll bet you don't," I told her savagely. Hell, I was in a mood and no mistake. "But, woman, you better think of something to say. Else I'm going out that door in about a minute and I ain't coming back."

"But—" she said.

I said, "Oh, god damnit! Quit mealymouthing around. Talk up like you got a little sand. Damnit!"

"But I can't!" she said. And be goddamn if she didn't kind of sob. "This is all I got. *This* is all the living I got. I can't run off from it just because you say to. How do I know?"

"Listen," I said, my voice still kind of savage, "don't talk to me about *knowing*. Nobody ever knows. They ain't no sure locks except four aces or a royal flush. I been spendin' the better balance of my life not knowing nothin'. And if that's good enough for me it goddamn well better be good enough for you. I been takin' chances all my life and if I can do it so can you. You come to this goddamn pig farm with your husband. You reckon that wasn't a chance? What the hell you call the mess you're in if not a chance?"

"But it's all I got!" she kind of wailed.

"Listen!" I said, and I whipped my revolver out of its holster and held it in the air and showed it to her. "That's all I got. That and a belief in myself and I'm still walking around free and doing a hell of a lot better than you. Don't talk to me about knowing. Don't talk to me about knowing the future. Ain't nobody knows that. Not nobody! I just do the best with what I got." I lowered my voice. "And right now I'm the best you got. And make no mistake. When I come on this place you was on your last legs and about to go under. Now you are making something of a hill climb. But, and I swear this, when I leave and you don't leave with me, you'll rot in a very short time."

She was starting to cry now. Just quiet little sobs that didn't have any force behind them. She was looking at me the whole time. "Oh, Mister Wilson," she said.

I said, "Don't goddamn well call me *Mister*! Damnit! I ain't your goddamn hideback husband who was raised on a rock farm in east Texas. I'm Wilson Young, not some pig farmer!"

She was trying to choke her sobs back, but not having much success. She asked me, her voice shaking, "But why can't you stay here with me and make a place out of this?"

I looked at her like she'd gone crazy. "Are you meaning what you say after what I've told you? You think I'd ruin myself fighting this land and this cold and watching you and me get old? For goddamn what? What?"

She was crying out loud now. "Fer a living!" she said.

I looked at her kind of cold. "I ain't interested in just making a living. If I'd wanted that I'd been a working for the other man a long time ago. And as for this"—and I kind of waved my hand around—"I don't call this no living."

She was crying, putting her hand up to her face every now and then. I wanted to reach over and comfort her a little, but I was damned if I would. Any woman that was going with me was going to be able to put up with some hardships and not fold when it got a little tough.

She kind of half screamed at me, "Then work for that ranch 'till we can make it better. That would be ar'right. Just work for them and see me when you can 'till we can get a bit put aside."

I said, "Woman, you are still not talking to Wilson Young. I don't work for nobody except me." My voice got very cold. I said, "Listen, I know the kind you need. They's a man that runs that ranch. His name is Ormsby. He dresses in good clothes and has got the kind of manners that women appreciate. Plus he don't take no chances for the money he makes. He works for a big outfit and the outfit is big enough that his little mistakes don't make no difference." My voice started rising. "Well, let me tell you, in my profession them little mistakes can get you killed. So what you need is a man like Ormsby who gets paid by that big ranch. He's like you; he holds on to what he can see. Me, I'm a fool to this world and always have been! All I got I can't see. Because it's just me and my courage and my belief in myself! So why don't you look up *Mister* Ormsby and fuck him like you do me and you'll be set for life! He's more yore kind!"

I left her at the table crying and walked over and kind of tipped my head against the wall. I was that disgusted. Disgusted with both her and me.

I tell you, it's tough on an outlaw. An outlaw tries to make his own way, but they are steadily getting themselves involved with those that don't have that kind of courage. The kind of courage it takes, like Chulo had, to just walk in and say, *"Cómo no?"*

It's those little careful people that always get an outlaw killed off.

But then she said, "Oh, Will!" And I looked over and she had her face against the tabletop and was crying. Hell, it just went through my heart so I went on back to the table and sat down. I wouldn't touch her. This was not the kind of medicine we were making where talk was good. This was the kind of medicine you make when you mean it and touching, between a man and a woman, interferes with that.

I said, "What?" I wanted to be kind of easy on her, but it still came out gruff.

She said, her face still against the table, "Why must you go?"

"Because," I said, and I got up and walked a pace away from the table and put my hands in the pockets of my breeches and said, "Because I must. Because I'm going to do a robbery here and I will have to flee for my life, and if you want to go with me you will have to go on your own."

I said it very coldly. It made her raise her face from the table and look at me. She was pale. "A robbery?"

"Yes," I said.

She kind of wailed. "Oh, no. But you're still an outlaw."

That made me angry again. I stalked toward her. I leaned over the table. "Yes, I'm still an outlaw. And I always will be. And if you go with me you'll be going as an outlaw's woman. Think on that!"

"But it can't be!" she said, and started crying again.

"Oh, hell!" I said, disgusted. Then I came back to the table. I raised my voice to her. She lifted her head. I jerked my head toward the north wall of the cabin. "What the hell you think that fence is up there except an outlaw? They are stealing from you except you don't call that goddamn ranch an outlaw. No, they do it different. They do it with money, with power. With all the goddamn tricks the law allows. You like that fence? Does anybody around here like that fence?"

She looked kind of uncertain. She finally said, "Well, no, but they leave us enough grazing to make it."

I looked at her, getting more and more angry and wishing I weren't. "Oh, goddamn!" I said. I walked over to the fire, looked in it for a minute, and then came back to her. "Listen, Hester," I said. I was starting to settle down a bit. "Listen, they are robbing you just as surely as I've robbed money with my revolver. The only difference is they call it business. You asked what I knew about old man Sutter? I know he's a man I can respect. I know he's a man who won't stand for having what's his robbed off him. Well, that's the kind of man I'd never rob. But I've been robbed and I intend to rob in return."

I sat down and then we sat there for a long time without a word passing between us.

After a long time I said, "Hester, I'm going my own way. Are you coming?"

Her head was back down. Finally she raised it. "What if I do? What if I quit this place to come with you? How will I know if you'll be in Amarillo to meet me?"

I looked at her. My voice got harsh. I didn't like that kind of thinking, not in the hazardous profession I was in. "And how will you know if lightning won't strike you tonight?"

"What?"

I leaned toward her. "Or how do you know the horse won't kick you when you go to hitch him up to meet me? Or how do you know you won't starve to death on this range when I leave? How the hell do you know anything for sure?" Hell, I was plenty disgusted with that kind of woman's talk. "Or how the hell, when I'm waiting and looking for you in Amarillo, in peril from the sheriff's office, do I know that you'll be there? How the hell do I know about you? Or about what you'll do? How the hell do I know you won't freeze to death between here and Amarillo? How the hell do I know you won't ride into Tascosa and tell the sheriff you know where Wilson Young is and he's fixing to pull a robbery?" Hell, I just got up and walked away from the table. Let her figure it out for herself. All she wanted was sureties. Which was just like a woman. Well, I didn't have any to offer.

Not being a big-shot businessman who spent most of his time cringing in his boots.

I started taking off my coat and then my shirt. I was going to bed. It was too late to go out in that cold and ride back to the line shack.

She was watching me.

I said, "All right, I got you one of them sure things. Stay on this godforsaken plains and rot."

Then I took off my gunbelt, laid it beside the bed, took off my boots and my trousers, and went on to bed. Sometime later on she crawled in over me, but I never paid her no mind.

The cabin was warm next morning when I got up. She already had a fire built and was fixing my breakfast. I got out of bed without a word, washed my face and mouth in the bucket and then put on my clothes and sat down at the table. She served me breakfast, bacon and beans and biscuits. She saw my mood and didn't say a word. While I was eating I was thinking about what had been said the night before and it made me plenty disgusted. Here she was in the fix she was in and I offer her a better way and she still wants suretys. How do I know if this will happen? How do I know if that will happen? Hell, she reminded me of someone standing out in the cold, freezing to death, and you invite them in to get warm by the fire and they say, "No, not unless you can guarantee me the fire won't go out."

Goddamn, that made me angry. Well, then let her stay on that poor-ass ranch and rot.

But she came up and sat down. I didn't look at her. I'd finished eating and was drinking a last cup of coffee and smoking a cigarillo. She said, "Will, I'll go with you."

"That ain't what I heard last night."

"I want to go with you." She reached out and tried to touch my hand, but I pulled it back.

"Don't do me no favors," I said.

"Oh, Will," she said. She pushed her hair back on the side like she always done. "Will, please."

I got up and started putting on my coat. "I'll see you in three days. Right now I got to git." I started for the door, but she jumped to the stove and said, "Wait, I fixed you yore noon meal."

I stopped just long enough to take it and stuff it in the pocket of my big coat. I said, "You think on it. Be sure it's a sure thing. I wouldn't want you to run off from your living."

Then I went out the door and to the shed and saddled my horse. When I rode away she was standing in the open door leaning up against the jamb. It was cold and there was a wind blowing and she ought not to have been taking a chance like that. She might have caught cold. Well, I'd see, in three days hence, if she still wanted to go. I felt bad leaving her like that, but I had to see if she could stand up and take a little rough treatment and still be sure.

Because if she went with me she was going to need all the tough she had.

But two nights later something very bad happened and it plumb wiped her out of my mind.

Wilcey and I had both come in from our patrols and were in the midst of eating supper when the door opened and Chulo came in. I looked at him and shook my head. "Oh, hell, here's the nigger Meskin. Get out of here before I stick a tamale up yore ass."

But he didn't laugh. He just stood there looking more serious than I'd ever seen him. Wilcey and I both looked at him and I knew something was wrong. I said, "Chulo, what the hell is it?"

He said, "*Chumacho*, they have killed your partner. They have killed the Preacher."

Chapter Six

Wilcey and I didn't say anything for a minute. We all three were just there, staring at each other. Finally Wilcey kind of croaked out, "What do you mean they killed him? Who killed him?"

Chulo untied the scarf under his chin and took off his hat. Then he stamped his feet, trying to work the cold out of them. He said, "That man Weelson spoke of. That Gaines."

I just sat there, staring at him. I'd lost another partner. Goddamn, I was hard on partners.

But Wilcey was asking, "How? Why?"

"*Quién sabe?*" he said. Who knows? "It was in that saloon where the Preacher played at poker. Gaines was playing and there was some words and then this Gaines kills hem." He shrugged and started taking off his coat.

I said, "You sure it was Gaines, Chulo?"

"*Seguro*," he said. He came over to the table and poured himself a cup of whiskey and sipped at it. "Jes, I went to the saloon when I heard. Gaines was still there. The sheriff said it was all right he shot the Preacher. The Preacher had a *pistolero*."

Wilcey said, "Of course, what else would you expect? That ranch owns the law."

"Well, they don't own me," I said. I got up and starting putting on my gunbelt. Wilcey looked up at me as I reached for my coat.

He said, "Where the hell are you going?"

I was buttoning my coat, looking down at the buttons. I said, "Going to kill Gaines."

"Tonight?"

"Right now," I said. I wasn't feeling much of nothing. I just didn't much like the idea of a *pistolero* killing my partner. My partner who couldn't have defended himself in a fair fight with a schoolboy.

Wilcey got up. "Will, wait! Let's talk about this."

"Ain't got time," I said. "I want to catch him while he's still in town. And I don't think he would have rode back to that ranch tonight."

I started to put on my hat, but Wilcey reached out and grabbed my arm. "Now, hold on, Will. We got to figure this out."

I jerked loose. "I done figured it out." Then I put on my hat and started toward the door, but Wilcey got in front of me. "Get out of my way, Wilcey," I told him.

He had me by both arms. "No, I ain't going to get out of your way. You are going to sit down here and we're going to talk this out."

"Goddamn you, Wilcey, I don't want to hurt you. Now, move!"

But he wouldn't so I commenced to shove him aside. He was not as strong as I was, but he was hanging on. I figured he'd lost his goddamn mind and I was about to fling him in the corner when he hollered for Chulo and then the black Mexican came over and commenced helping him. We struggled back and forth. I couldn't fling them off and they couldn't back me into the chair they were trying to get me in. Strangely enough I wasn't angry. I wasn't feeling much of anything except a sincere desire to kill Gaines. And I was going to kill that no good chickenshit two-bit cocksucking afterbirth-eating sonofabitch.

And no mistake.

While we struggled Wilcey kept talking to me.

"Take it easy, Will."

"I'm going to kill him."

"I know, but not now."

"I'm going to kill him."

"Will, I can't lose two partners. I don't want you to get killed."

"I'll kill him."

"I know you'll kill Gaines, but then they'll kill you. If you kill him now you'll be running penniless. Kill him in the robbery."

"I'm going to kill him tonight."

"You can't do that. If you kill him in town you'll be lucky to get a half a mile. This is their territory. Wait!"

I could hear them panting. I was panting myself. Wilcey said, "Goddamn, hit him with something, Chulo!"

Chulo said, "*Amigo, por favor, dispénseme! Por favor!*"

"He knew the Preacher was my partner. He's trying to get at me. The motherfucker!"

Chulo said, "Leesten to Weelcey."

"Turn me loose, you sonofabitches!" I said, but without any heat in it. "I'm gonna kill him. And I'm gonna kill him tonight."

And then all of a sudden Wilcey stepped back and slapped me in the face. I was so startled I stopped struggling and just stood there staring at him.

His face was red, the way it gets when he's angry. He said, "Just who the goddamn hell you think you are? You forgetting Preacher was my friend too? And my partner? Who the hell gave you the right to kill Gaines? I got just as much right as you do! You sonofabitch!"

I just stared at him. He'd startled me so that I was just standing there. Chulo even dropped his hands, knowing I wasn't going anywhere.

Wilcey was mad as hell. He said, "I agree you ought to kill him because you got the best chance and because he was trying to get at you through the Preacher. You and him been eyein' each other like two bulls ever since that night in the saloon. But I be goddamn if you going in and kill him like this and git yo'self kilt in the bargain. No, sir! No, by God, sir, you ain't! I ain't fixin' to lose *two* partners in the same night!"

Well, he was giving me pause.

He was going on. He said, "Kill him, but kill him in the robbery. Kill him then when we'll have their gold and will have a good chance to make a getaway. Kill him then. Kill him in cold blood. Shoot him down like a dog! Shoot him in the back. Give him the same chance he gave the Preacher, which was none!"

"Oh, shit," I said. I turned away and went over and sat down at the table and poured myself out a drink of whiskey, but I didn't touch it. Instead I took off my hat and my coat and then my gunbelt. Then I sat back down, sat there with that cup in front of me. They just stood there staring at me. Finally I uncorked the bottle and poured out two more cups.

Then they came over and sat down. We just sat there, not drinking, not speaking, the whiskey sitting in front of us. Chulo lit a cigarillo and I lit one and then we sat there smoking, for how long I don't know.

Finally I reached out and took up my tin cup of whiskey. Wilcey and Chulo did the same. I lifted mine in the air and they followed me.

"To the Preacher," I said. "I never knowed his proper name, but this one is good enough."

"Neither did I," Wilcey said. "To the Preacher."

Chulo said, "To the Preacher. *Vaya con Dios con bueno suerte.*"

So we toasted him and did what we could to lay him to rest. Hell, I ain't much of a crying man, but I reckon one of my eyes got a little something in it. I said, "Shit!" and spit on the floor.

Well, we didn't have much to say after that. Wilcey poured out all around again and we sat there sipping whiskey and thinking our own thoughts. Of course Chulo was an outsider where the Tinhorn had been concerned, but he was *simpático* enough to understand how me and Wilcey felt.

I said, "Well, I kind of blame myself for this. If I hadn't gotten him involved in that holdup of that poker game he might never have got to thinking of himself as a gunhand."

Wilcey said, "Aw, bullshit, Will. That wasn't yore doin'. Hell, we kept telling him—you kept telling him he wasn't no good with a gun. Hell, you can't blame yourself for that."

Chulo said, "The way of it was this Gaines was playing at the poker with the Preacher and he called the Preacher a cheat and said they would go out to the street and settle the matter. Only—"

"Shit!" I said. "There it is right there. The Preacher would never have had to cheat to beat Gaines or any of them other waddies for that matter. That was just an excuse."

"As you say," Chulo said. "But they never got to the street. When the Preacher stood up, Gaines shot him. The Preacher did not have his weapon in his hand, but the law, they say he is carrying one so he is armed, and this Gaines only acts in self-defense."

"Well," I said, "I'm going to be sure Mister Gaines has a pistol. But I don't believe they'll call it self-defense."

Wilcey suddenly laughed. I looked around at him wondering what he found so goddamn funny at such a time. He said, "I just got to thinking about old Preacher getting up from that table. I bet that silly sonofabitch was really intending to go outside and shoot it out with Gaines."

Well, it made me kind of smile, too. We kind of got to talking about him then, telling Chulo stories on him. Wilcey told the one about how after we'd fled to California the Preacher had bought himself a fancy gun rig and we used to catch him practicing with it in his hotel room.

"Oh, hell," Wilcey said, laughing, "that was the scardest sonofabitch you ever saw when we went in on that poker-game robbery. But six months later you'd almost have thought, way he talked, that he'd done it single-handedly. I never could make him understand that it was Will they was scairt of and not him. And then we pulled a few more jobs in California and, ever' time, he was scairt to death going in, but swelled up like a pouter pigeon afterward. Hell, we got to calling him Jesse James there for a while."

"He didn't start out that a'way," I said. I told them the first time I'd seen the Tinhorn. I said, "I was playing in a little two-bit game in a saloon in Del Rio and this one in the game looked about as much like a tinhorn gambler down on his luck as anything you've ever seen—plug hat, frock coat, and them stovepipe breeches—but all of them looking just a bit seedy and frayed around the edges. Anyway, I didn't pay much attention to him except to note he was a pretty good poker player. But, hell, anybody can be a good poker player in a two-bit game. Then, next day I was taking a little dinner at this café and he come up and sat down at my table. Uninvited. And wanted to know if I knew where there was a bigger game. Well, there was this government casino across the border in Villa Acuana and—"

Wilcey said, "I've played there."

And Chulo stroked his black handlebar moustache

and said, "Ah, I too. But not the poker. The wheeskey and the wemen."

"Anyway, I told him about it and he wanted to know if I was going and could he go with me. I told him, 'Hell, no.' I didn't know when I was going and I damn sure didn't want to be bothered with no goddamn tinhorn. I told him just cross the International Bridge and head for the noise and lights. Couldn't miss it. Well, I went on over after a time and, pretty soon, who comes sliding in but the Tinhorn. Sit down at the same game I was in, which kind of surprised me because we was playing some serious poker. Well, we done pretty good. Funny thing was old Preacher started driving this rich Mexican ranch owner up to me. Just herding him right on up. After I figured out what he was doing I went to returning the favor and we whipsawed that old boy back and forth pretty good. When it was over I went over to the bar and got me a bottle of brandy and sat down, thinking I'd have me a quiet drink or two. But here comes the Tinhorn. Well, wasn't much I could do except shove him out a chair and invite him to a drink. We jawed awhile and then I got ready to leave. I'd won about a thousand and I reckon he had too. I told him I was going to *adiós* the place and he wondered if he couldn't walk back with me. Said he'd won a pretty good little piece of change and he was kind of nervous about them Mexican *banditos*."

I give Chulo a wink and said, "Eh, Nigger?"

He pulled one eye.

I said, "Well, I told him he could walk back with me, but I damn well wasn't riding shotgun for nobody. That if he got into a mess that was his lookout. He thought that'd be all right so we started to leave. Just as we went out the door something suddenly struck me and I turned around and asked him what made him think *I* wouldn't rob him. He said, 'Oh, sir, you don't look like a robber!' "

Well, that give us all a pretty good laugh.

Wilcey said, shaking his head, "That silly sonofabitch."

We got quiet after that. I guess it would be awhile before we realized old Preacher was really dead. So I guess we were doing the best we could, drinking and laughing and telling stories on him. But all I could keep thinking about was him thinking enough of me to bring me those canned apricots and peaches.

Oh, goddamn, was I going to kill Joe Gaines.

It was pretty late when we finally went to bed. I told Chulo to go on back into town next morning and gather up all his gear and come back to the line camp. I figured he might as well stay with us the rest of the time, the robbery being only three days away now.

Next morning, after breakfast, I told Wilcey to give that five-mile patrol a sort of lick and a promise. I said, "I don't reckon we'll be too much more concerned with our wage-paying jobs from here on in." Then I told Chulo not to get back too early for fear a checkup rider might come by and spot him. I told him also to bring back about a dozen quarts of whiskey, since we were commencing to get low.

I told them both. "I've got a little piece of business to take care of today and tonight I won't be back. So look for me about noon tomorrow."

Wilcey said to Chulo, "Wilson's got him a woman."

Chulo laughed. "*Mi amigo siempre tiene una señorita.*"

"You ignorant meskin," I said. "Wilcey don't speak Spanish. And you in the *Estados Unidos*. Speak English." I said to Wilcey, "He just said, in Spanish, that I was hell with the women."

Which made Chulo laugh. He waved his finger

back and forth. "Oh, no, no, no. I say *mi amigo* has *mucho* trouble with the weemen."

"That's about the straight of it," Wilcey said dryly. "Ever since I've known him."

Not too much later we all rode out, each on different errands. I headed south and a little east, aiming for old man Sutter's place. Only directions I had was him pointing and saying six miles, but I reckoned I could find it. Hell, on that bald-ass prairie if you got within a mile of something bigger than a flattopped rock you could spot it easy. I'd thought of stopping at Hester's place to get directions, but I thought I'd get this piece of business done and see her on the way back.

I raised what I took to be Sutter's place after about an hour-and-a-half ride. It was a sod house, but it had a good set of corrals out back and was about as well-tended as a place could be in that sorry country. I came galloping up, then slowed my horse to a walk and finally stopped about ten yards from the house. A bunch of cur dogs came boiling out from the back, yapping and barking their fool heads off. There was no one in sight outside so I halloed the house.

"Hallooo the house!" I yelled.

Nothing happened for a moment and then the door opened and a woman stood there wiping her hands on her apron, just looking at me without saying a word. I touched my hat to her. It was a cold morning, but it wasn't uncommonly cold and it was clear. I said, "Morning, Ma'am. I'm looking for old man Sutter."

She didn't say anything so I said, "Got a business proposition for him. Ain't bringing trouble."

About that time one of them moon-faced boys of his popped up over her shoulder. I said "Howdy. Yore paw at home? Want to talk a little business with him."

Then they all scattered and Sutter came to the door.

He had on his britches and his boots and his undershirt, but no coat and no hat.

"Howdy, Sutter," I said, "remember me?"

"I recollect," he said. "If you come for trouble I sure hope you brought yoreself a noon meal. Like I told you."

I shook my head. "No. I ain't here about the fence. I got a private matter of business I want to discuss."

He studied me a long moment.

I said, "It'll put money in your pocket."

"Get down," he said. "And come in."

I climbed off my horse and one of his boys came rushing out to take the reins from me. Then I clumped on inside the cabin, stamping my feet to warm them up. That was the hell of that country, a man's feet damn near froze in the stirrups.

The inside was smoky from a cow-chip fire, but it was warm and pretty well fixed up. It was bigger than Hester's shack, but built about the same.

Sutter was standing by the table. He took a chair and indicated one to me. "Set, if you be a mind."

"Thanks." I dropped in it and his wife brought me over a cup of coffee. I looked over at Sutter. "How's your cattle doing?"

"They be all right," he said.

His wife and his two moon-faced boys were standing around gawking at us. I said, "Let me get right down to it. I'd like to bring four—no, I mean, three horses over here and leave them tomorrow for a couple of days."

"Why be ye wanting to do that?"

"My reasons are my own, Mister Sutter. But I'll pay you and pay you well for this."

"If this be that ranch's bidness, the answer is no. And ye can tell them sorry bosses of yoren that Amos Sutter says they can rot in hell."

I half laughed. "This ain't the ranch's business. I can guarantee you that."

"Well, I ain't holdin' with no bidness with that damn ranch."

"I said it ain't the ranch's business, and it ain't. Look here, ain't I played pretty square with you?"

"Mebbe so," he said.

"All right then. Do me this boon. I want to bring three horses up here and leave them in your care. Then in a couple of days me and my two partners will be coming by here to pick them up."

He shook his head. "That's mighty outlandish."

"Damnit, Sutter," I said, getting a little impatient. "They's a hundred dollars in gold in it for you."

Well, that made him wall his eyes a little.

I said, "Is it a deal?"

"No, sir!" he said. "Noooo, sir!" He got up from the table. "Any man willin' to pay a hunnert dollars for the upkeep of three horses for two days is up to devilment and me and mine won't take no part in it. Noooo, sir!"

"Sutter," I said. "It's not the ranch's business. I don't really work for that ranch. It's just been a place for me to hide out and I ain't give a damn if every cow in this territory goes through that fence. I'm a robber by trade."

Well, it was worth it. I'd been trying to get a rise out of that old man from the first day I'd seen him. I couldn't scare him with my guns, nor with my threats, but I'd finally made him go slack-jawed. He stared at me and then he stared at his wife and his moon-faced boys and then came back to me.

"That's right, Sutter," I said. "I'm going to do a robbing. And that's why I want fresh horses ready here. When we get to yore place the ones we'll be on will be nearly ridden out and we want some fresh ones ready and waiting."

He said, still staring at me, "Well, I be goldarned!"

I reckoned I was the first robber he'd ever seen, or at least the first one that admitted to it. He was still staring at me. "That's right, Sutter. Just what your ears heard. Is it a deal? I got to be getting along."

He said, "Who—who you be going to rob?"

"None of your business," I said.

"Ye ain't going to rob the poor, be ye?"

"Sutter, is your head made of oak wood? If I was going to rob somebody poor, how the hell could I afford to give you a hundred dollars for tending horses?"

He kind of mumbled something.

I said, "What?"

He cleared his throat and looked at his old woman. Then he looked back at me. "Onliest ones in this part of the country with any cash money is that ranch. Ye be going to rob that ranch?"

"Yes," I said, looking at him.

"Glory be," he said. "Galooory be!"

His wife said, "Hallelujah!"

"Then it's a deal?"

"You mighty right, mister. You mighty right. Ye bring yore horses on an' they will be as tended as stock kin be tended. An' they'll be a-settin' here waitin' when ye comes through."

"Be sure of that," I said. "Because when we come we are going to be in a hurry."

"They be waitin'."

I'd taken a hundred dollars off of Chulo the night before and I reached in my pocket and spun a twenty-dollar gold piece on the table. "Then take that to seal the bargain."

He looked at the gold piece and then at me. Finally he reached out and put his hand on it. He said, "I be going to take it for I need it for maw and the boys. But iffen I didn't need it I wouldn't take it, not for nothin', not for hurt against the goldarn ranch. But that be enough. They'll be no more talk about a hunnert dollars."

"A bargain is a bargain," I said.

"No, sir," he said. "Nooo, sir!"

I laughed and got up from the table. "All right, Sutter. I'll be here tomorrow with the horses."

"They be tended," he said.

I made my good-byes and then went on outside. One of the boys ran and brought me my horse. When I was mounted I looked at Sutter. "Good luck," I told him.

"Jesus be with ye," he said.

I tipped my hat and rode off, heading for Hester's place.

Chapter Seven

I reckoned she saw me through the window as I came riding up, for she came to the door as I headed for the shed to put my horse up. I got him unsaddled, gave him some grain, and then went on into the house. She was at the stove as I came in. I sat down at the table without a word and she turned from the stove, her face flushed from either the heat or something else. She said, "Yore nooning be ready in a minute."

"Fine," I said. "Bring me a cup of that sweet juice off them apricots or peaches."

After she opened the can she poured it off in a tin cup and brought it over to me. I'd left a bottle of whiskey on the table and I poured a good dose of that in the juice and then sat there sipping it, watching her bustling around the stove. She'd made a beef stew and she served me up a bowl of it. I ate it along with cold biscuits and coffee. She still wouldn't eat with me, but she did sit down across the table. I could see she'd got herself up extra pretty.

She said, a little nervously, "I hoped you'd like stew. I made it for you."

I said, "It's mighty savory." And it was. It had potatoes and wild onions in it and was rich and thick.

She ran her hand through her hair. "I was afeered you might not come," she said.

"Why's that?" I asked her.

She gave a kind of nervous little laugh. "Oh, I don't know. You kind of had your back up when you left. And you didn't kiss me good-bye."

"I said I'd be back."

Then I ignored her until I was finished eating. Finally I shoved my plate back and lit a cigarillo while she brought me another cup of coffee. I said, "Well, you still feel the same way?"

She kind of ducked her head real quick and said, "Yes. But I'm scairt."

"Scared? What are you scared of?"

"Well," she said, "I got to thinking last night I hadn't knowed you very long. Maybe not even a month."

"I've gone on robberies with men I haven't even known a week. Trusted them with my life. One of the worst double crosses I've ever had was from a man I'd known for years. Time ain't got a goddamn thing to do with it."

"Still," she said, "I'm still scairt." She paused and looked away from me. "But I'd be more scairt to stay here with you gone."

"I got to tell you something. It may make you change your mind."

She looked suddenly a little afraid. "Oh, Lord, don't let it be nothin' real bad."

"I'm going to do murder."

She looked confused. "I don't understand. I thought you told me you'd killed before."

"In a fair fight, yes. But I've never done murder before. Now I'm going to shoot a man down in cold blood, without giving him a chance."

She no more knew what I was talking about than the man in the moon. She said, "Well, why are you going to do it?"

"Because the man killed my partner. And he's an

experienced gunman and my partner wasn't. I'm going to give him the same chance he gave my partner—none."

"Oh," she said, "Oh, I see."

Well, it didn't matter that she didn't understand. At least she didn't disapprove. I wasn't looking for her approval, or anyone else's for that matter, but I did want her to know.

I said, "You understand you've got to leave day after tomorrow morning. At first light. And you've got to go just as hard as you can all day long. If you run across a cabin or a ranch where there's a wife, you might try to get shelter for the night. Other than that, sleep in your buggy, but tether your horse to one of the wheels. Don't worry about him grazing; take along plenty of grain."

She kind of raised her chin. "Mister Young," she said. "I believe I can undertake to get myself to Amarillo on time. You needn't instruct me like I was Ned in the first primer."

Well, it made me laugh a little. "All right," I said, "but they's some other things you need to know. I—oh, before I forget." I reached in my pocket and got forty dollars in gold coin and put them on the table. "You may need that in Amarillo. When I get there I'll give you more for the long trip you've got after that. Now, what you do," I said, "as soon as you get to Amarillo, and you ought to get there about noon of the second day, is you go and put your horse in a livery stable and then go to the train depot and sit down there and wait for me to get there. Just stay right there until I show up, else I won't know where to find you and my time in Amarillo is going to be mighty short. I ought to be there no later than that night. Because we won't stop for anything. If I'm not there by the next morning, just go and get your buggy hitched up and head on back to this place because it'll mean, if I don't show up, that I'm either killed or bad shot and—"

She kind of drew in her breath and started to say something, but I held my hand up. "If you're going to be hitched to me you might's well make up your mind right now that, the way I earn my living, there's always the chance of getting killed or captured, and that's just part of it. So don't start no wailing about it. Now, from there you're going to have a long train ride. I'll be there to get your ticket for you and tell you what to do."

"Where we be going?"

"Del Rio."

"Del Rio? Where in the world is that?"

"Right down on the Mexican border. It's about five hundred miles south of Amarillo."

"My stars!" she said. "Near Mexico! That'll be the furtherest I ever been. And we're going on the train all the way?"

"No. You're going on the train. Me and my two partners will travel over land a-horseback. They'd spot me immediately on a train. When you get to Del Rio you're going to go to the Cattleman's Hotel and I'll meet you there in about two weeks."

"You mean I won't see you for two weeks? I'll be there by myself for two weeks?"

"How long you been by yourself out here on this prairie?"

She didn't say anything.

"You'll have plenty of money and you'll be all right. Just be goddamn sure you don't mention my name. Not to anybody."

I could see the excitement starting to work in her. She'd probably never even ridden a train before and now she was going all the way nearly to Mexico. It made me about half smile watching her face. Lord, she was beginning to look younger. The woman I'd first met had looked nearer to forty instead of the twenty this one was beginning to look like.

I said, "I've made a deal with old man Sutter to look after your stock. So don't worry about that."

"Stars," she said, shaking her head, "you do get around. You just keep my head in a whirl."

That was about all the details. We didn't do much the balance of the day except sit around. She went through her poor, meager belongings, trying to decide what she could take. I helped as best I could, pointing out that things like a big black kettle would be a burden on a train trip. She had only one old cloth valise, so I got her a couple of feed sacks out of the shed and brought them in for her to use. She was packing way too much, but it did me no good to say anything. I kept trying to tell her that she'd be able to buy all new stuff in her new home, but she couldn't quite take that in. I imagine that the $40 that was still lying on the table was the most cash money she'd ever had in her life.

The hardest thing to get her to leave was her hope chest, all the embroideries and what not that she'd made prior to her marriage. Hell, I think she wanted to take the chest itself, but I reckon she finally saw that was impossible. Well, I was just kind of staying out of it. She'd figure out, once she got to Amarillo, that there's just so much you can lug on a train. Besides, I imagine those things were a comfort to her, going into a strange new life as she was. I really couldn't blame her for being afraid. I asked her at one point what her dead husband had been like and she'd shrugged and said he'd been a good man, but that he'd been nothing like me.

"How's that?" I asked her.

"Well," she'd said, "he was, uh, sort of common. No,

I don't mean common as bad, he was just sort of what you might call everyday. And o' course you ain't. You're wild and kind of scary. I could feel the wildness in you the first night you come here."

We went to bed early and made a different kind of love for a long time. It wasn't so much fucking as it was just kind of holding on to each other. I wouldn't know what love is, the kind I've heard people talk about, if I'd had six schoolteachers explain it to me, but whatever it was we were doing was probably pretty close to that.

Next morning I ate breakfast without saying much. Didn't either one of us say anything. About all I said was, "If you run into anybody and they want to know where you're going, tell them you're going to Amarillo to be with your sister who is having a baby and needs yore help with the rest of the kids."

She just nodded.

After that I went to the shed and saddled my horse and then led him back up to the cabin. She was in the door. I kissed her, putting one arm around her kind of tightly. "See you in Amarillo," I said. Then I mounted and would have rode off, but she came up to me and put her hand on my leg and looked up into my face. "Will," she said, "be careful."

"Oh, hell," I said, a little disgusted. "You could have gone all day without saying something like that. Do you think I got as old in this business as I have without knowing how to be careful?"

She looked down at the ground. "I reckon," she said. "It's just all so new. And I wanted to say something."

"I know," I said. I leaned way low and kissed her lightly on the lips. "Now I got to get. I'll see you in Amarillo. *Adiós* and *buena suerte*."

Then I reined around and went off at a gallop. I

had to get back to the line shack and collect our horses and take them to old man Sutter's.

Chulo was at the shack, but Wilcey was out, going through the motions of playing fence guard. Chulo helped me get our three good saddle horses together and load them with all the feed grain and supplies that we wouldn't need after the next couple of days. I figured Sutter would be gladder to see the flour and dried beans and canned goods than he would the money I was going to pay him.

When the horses were all ready I mounted up, told Chulo I'd be back in a few hours, and then took the stock on lead and set off for Sutter's.

Sutter was outside when I pulled up to the house. He was, indeed, grateful for the supplies. He and his moon-faced boys unloaded them and then turned our horses into a handy corral.

"Sonny," he said, "I don't be knowing yore name and I don't reckon you be wantin' me to know it. But I'm grateful for all ye've brung and we'll take it 'cause we can use it. And you can bet yore bottom dollar I'll keep my part of the bargain. When you be coming by for them horses?"

"Day after tomorrow," I said. "About mid-morning. And we're going to be in a hell of a hurry."

He nodded and spit. "Them horses will be fed and fresh watered and rested and standin' right 'chere in the front yard with my boys holdin' them when ye git here."

"Good enough." I mounted. "Oh, one other thing. Do you know the widow woman that lives up north a few miles?"

"Widder Hester?"

"That's the one. I saw her when I was riding over here and she asked me to ast you if you'd look after her stock for a few days. She's got a sister in Amarillo who's come to layin' in time and she's gone to help.

Guesses she'll be gone a week or ten days. Will you do that?"

"Why o' course."

I rode straight on back to the line camp, my route taking me very near Hester's place. I could have stopped in to see her, but it wasn't the time. Now was the time to forget her and everyone else and commence to concentrating on the job at hand.

Chapter Eight

I got up the next morning a little after daylight. There was no point in any of us getting up early. We weren't going to make any pretense about riding that fence. With the robbery the next day we didn't give a goddamn who came by. If the wrong person showed up he'd likely get his ass shot or tied up for a long time.

After breakfast, which was none too good because none of us was much interested in that right then, I walked outside in the cold wind and looked off to the southeast. By now Hester, if she was doing what she'd said she would, ought to have been a good number of miles on down the road to Amarillo. Well, I couldn't worry about that, right then. I had more pressing matters to tend my mind to.

We spent the balance of the day not saying much of anything to one another. I reckon there are outlaws and robbers who can go in on a job without a sign of nerves, but I ain't one of them. And neither is Wilcey nor Chulo.

Well, maybe Chulo. He didn't have anywhere near as bad a case as me and Wilcey. Wilcey's main concern seemed to be how I knew that the gold would be moved the next morning.

"Hell," I said, "I don't *know* for a fact they going to move that gold out there tomorrow morning. But since the next day is payday, they going to have a bunch of goddamn angry hired hands if they don't.

And that's what they been doing in the past, best the Preacher could find out, so why figure they'll do any different now?"

"Well, I just wanted to be sure."

"Sure? Then goddamn don't be asking me if you want to be sure. Because I don't know for sure. If you want to be real sure go and ask Ormsby or that little strutting major. They can tell you for sure! Shit!"

And we sat around cleaning our weapons and counting our cartridges and that kind of stuff, which was about as useful an enterprise as tits on a boar hog. Men in our line of work *always* have their weapons in top condition or they don't last very long.

I went over, for about the tenth time, what every man was to do and how he was to do it. I went over it so many times that even the gentle-tempered Chulo finally said, in exasperation, *"No más, no más! Por favor!"*

Wilcey said, "Shit, I'm so goddamn ready to get out of this country I'm about willing to go into town and blow that fucking bank up!"

"What do you mean, this country? This is your home range, remember?"

"Not any more," he said, meaning it. "I want to get back down to the border. I've had all this cold and snow and bald-ass prairie I want. I've had enough to last me a lifetime. I want out of here!"

Which made me think of Hester and the little-girl questions she'd asked me about the border the day before. She'd had a hard time understanding that it was warm all year round and they didn't have any snow. But worse than that was me trying to explain a watermelon or a cantaloupe to her. I didn't even bother to try her on a papaya. Hell, it was kind of funny.

Well, I was like Wilcey, only more so. I'd been too

long off my home range and I was more than ready to get back, no matter what the chances were.

Night came on and I walked outside and looked up at the sky. It was cold, but it was staying clear. I thought of Hester out there somewhere on that prairie, hoping maybe she'd have found shelter with some ranch family. But I wasn't going to worry. She'd said she knew what to do and, hell, she'd lived alone for a good many months. I'd just have to figure she could make it. I had enough to worry about on my own.

The evening kind of dragged on. We ate some supper, but wasn't any of us really hungry except Chulo, who ate about three bowls of beans and a bunch of biscuits and some canned goods. We didn't want too much weighing us down.

Wilcey and I played some head-up poker while Chulo, who didn't play, watched. It didn't last long because neither one of us could keep his mind on the game. We finally threw our hands in and then just sat around drinking whiskey and thinking.

"Shit," Wilcey said, "I wish it was morning. Goddamn, I'll be glad to get out of this place."

Which showed how nervous we were all getting.

We finally went on to bed, Chulo spreading his bedroll on the floor. I lay there that night listening to the wind howl and whistle through the chinks in the walls, not thinking about much of anything, just kind of idly wondering how it was all going to come out. But I'd been down the trail so often I'd begun to believe nothing could happen to me.

And, of course, as soon as you start thinking that way, that's when you get yours.

We got up before dawn. My best guess was they'd be leaving Tascosa with that payroll gold not too many minutes after eight o'clock, and I wanted to be well in position and waiting for them.

We all got up and made breakfast without anybody saying much of nothing. It was hard to eat with a jumpy stomach, but we all forced down as much as we could, knowing we'd be riding hard after the robbery and wouldn't have any time to stop and eat. After that we saw to the horses, making sure they were well grained and watered. They were company horses, and not of the best, but we were going to give them a hard run.

After that we all sat around a few minutes drinking a little coffee and whiskey. I watched the window, watching the false dawn break.

"Anybody want any more whiskey?" Nobody said anything so I plugged the jug, poured out the coffee, and started loading saddlebags. "It's time," I said. "Roll up your sleeping gear and get your other truck."

We saddled and bridled the horses and then loaded on what little provisions we were taking. Then we mounted up. We had good light by then. We sat there a moment in front of the line shack. "Well," I said, "we've seen the last of this place."

Wilcey said, "Yeah, one way or the other."

I looked at him sharply. "That's bad luck talk, Wilcey. Don't ever go in on a job thinking like that."

Then we reined around and started south for the intersection of that ranch road and the Canadian River. I figured it to be about six miles, maybe a little better. It ought not to take us more than half an hour. Maybe fifteen minutes longer. We'd be there in plenty of time.

Nobody said much of anything on that ride. I was glad to see the sky was staying clear. I damn sure wouldn't have wanted to see any blizzard blowing up.

Wilcey said, "I just hope to hell they show up."

"Goddamn, Wilcey, take it easy. It's going to turn out all right. You worry too much to make a self-respecting bandit."

But my own stomach was jumping around all to hell.

I halted us once, got a bottle of whiskey out of my saddlebags, and we all had a good slug.

"For the cold," I said.

Chulo grinned. "Sure. For the cold."

We went on and hit the road and then turned left toward Tascosa. After about ten minutes we rose the little line of trees that marked the Canadian River. We rode on up to it. There was no sign of anyone coming. I calculated it was right at eight o'clock. Ormsby and his party ought to be along in about half-to-three-quarters of an hour. At the river Wilcey and Chulo dismounted and led their horses back and hid them, on either side of the road, as best they could among the trees. They hid them about a hundred yards off the road. Then they came forward with their rifles and hid themselves in the rocks. They were positioned so that they'd have the drop on Ormsby's bunch just as his party came out of the river-crossing. I rode down the road a ways toward Tascosa to see if I could see anybody coming, but the road was empty as far as I could see. I turned back, looking to see how well hidden Chulo and Wilcey and their horses were. They were about as well hidden as could be and a man would have to be looking for them to see 'em.

"All right," I said, as I passed by them, *"Buena suerte."*

Then I rode on up the road a good half mile, finding me a little rise to get a better view, turned to face Tascosa, and then just settled down to wait.

After a few minutes I commenced to get cold. I twisted around and got the whiskey out of my saddlebags and had a pull, reflecting that Chulo and Wilcey were probably pretty cold themselves. But at least they were down out of the wind. I put the bottle back and lit a cigarillo. My horse began to stamp his feet.

"Take it easy, horse," I said, "I don't like this standing and waiting any better than you do, but they ain't nothing else we can do."

I tell you the waiting was forever. I don't know if it was as long as it seemed, but it seemed like an hour. Just as I began to think Wilcey's worst fears were about to come true I saw some little dots top a rise coming out of Tascosa. I held my breath as they came on, hoping against hope. Then, in a few minutes, I could make out a buckboard drawn by one horse and four outriders. Well, that sure fit the description of what I was waiting on.

My heart began to beat rapidly and my mouth went dry. I reckon there are those whose mouth don't get dry before a job, but I ain't one of them. I was getting plenty tensed up and no mistake. I got my revolver out of its holster and shoved it inside my coat, into the waist of my breeches. I kept my hand in there, holding it by the butt.

I watched the oncoming party, gauging their progress. I didn't want to get to the river before them; I wanted to arrange to meet them right between Wilcey and Chulo. So, when it looked right, I started my horse forward, very slowly. I rode hunched over in the saddle with my hand inside my coat, trying to look like a man who'd been hurt bad.

They came on and the distance between us slowly narrowed. I stopped once to let them get a little closer to the river and also, now that they could probably see me a little better, to make it look like I was about to fall out of the saddle.

It was the only way I could think of where they'd let me get close enough to get the drop on them. The feel of the butt of my revolver was reassuring, but there were five of them and if some general shooting started I was almost certain to get hit.

Then they were entering the river. I stopped my

horse about twenty yards from the water's edge, staying hunched in the saddle. I didn't know if they recognized me or if they weren't afraid of one man, but they came on, the wheels of the buckboard throwing up little rooster trails of water. They emerged from the river and then stopped, just about where I'd wanted them to. I let my horse ease forward and, when I was about ten yards away, they all came up with their rifles and leveled down on me. I came on a few more yards and then kind of raised a little in the saddle.

"Mister Ormsby," I said. "I'm shot." I was trying to make my voice sound like I was dying. "A bunch jumped us at the fence this morning and kilt my partner and I near about didn't get away."

"Oh, goddamn!" Ormsby swore. "Who were they? What were they doing?"

"They was stealing Skillet cattle. They'd torn down a whole big piece of fence and was pushing near a thousand head south. Me and my partner done what we could, but they was too many of them."

I was gradually letting my horse ease forward. The guards had lowered their rifles and were listening to what I was saying. Gaines was on Ormsby's right and Sawyer was on his left. I didn't know the two in the back. Ormsby was driving the buckboard.

Ormsby was cussing a blue streak. "A thousand head you say? A thousand head! God almighty damn!"

"I'm shot Mister Ormsby. I got to get to a doctor."

I was still letting my horse ease forward. By then I was only a few yards away. I suddenly straightened and drew my revolver and said, "Hands up!"

One of the guards in the back, the one behind Sawyer, started up with his rifle and I shot him dead center in the chest, the power of the slug flipping him backward out of the saddle. I never paused to see the effect of my work, just swung straight on Gaines. But he wasn't moving; he was too experienced a hand for that.

"Now, drop them rifles and get your hands up! DROP THEM, GOD DAMNIT!"

Wilcey and Chulo were scrambling out of the ditch, their rifles leveled on the party. Sawyer let his go and then the other guard in the back did the same. Gaines didn't have one, only his side-gun. But Ormsby had one on the wagon seat beside him. I told him to kick it overboard. But before he could move Wilcey was there and he took it and slung it off the road.

Ormsby said, "Wilson, what the hell you think you're doing?"

"Hell, I'm robbing you. What the hell does it look like, you dumb sonofabitch! And my name ain't just Wilson. It's Wilson Young."

Gaines gave a little snort. "I thought I knew you."

"You ain't going to know me long," I told him.

With his hands in the air he told Ormsby, "You hired you a real ring-tailed cat, Mister Ormsby. This one is wanted in every county in Texas."

"Well, he won't get away with this." He said to me, "You sonofabitch, nobody robs the Skillet Ranch and gets away with it."

"Uh, huh," I said. "Keep talking, Ormsby."

Chulo and Wilcey were gathering up all the handguns and rifles and slinging them way off the road. We were working fast. It was unlikely anyone would come along, but we didn't want to take any more chances than necessary. Then Chulo dragged the strongbox off the back of the buckboard while Wilcey ran to get his horse. When he was mounted he galloped over and got Chulo's and brought it back.

The strongbox was secured with a padlock. Chulo shot it off and they opened it. The gold was there all right, an easy ten thousand dollars' worth. We didn't whoop and holler like greenhorns. We'd seen gold before. Chulo and Wilcey commenced to load it into our saddlebags, distributing it so that it wouldn't make too big a load in any one. When the saddlebags were tied on our horses I told our victims to dismount. "Get off your horses and Ormsby, get out of that wagon."

He'd been talking nonstop, cussing me steady. He started, "Listen, Wilson—"

And I cut him off. "Listen, you sonofabitch, you call me *Mister* Young. Wilson is only for my friends."

"The hell with you, I wouldn't call you mister. You are beneath my contempt."

"You're fixing to be beneath the ground if you don't get out of that wagon."

He didn't move and so Chulo hit him upside the head, knocking him over the side. He got up, blood streaming down his face. He wasn't cussing so fast any more.

Wilcey was busy, meanwhile, getting all the horses tied together on one lead rope. We were going to take them with us, at least for a mile or so.

They were all standing there with their hands in the air. Sawyer was off to my right a little and he sort of let his arms droop. I swung my gun on him. "Just do something, Sawyer. Anything. I'm dying to kill you. I bet that'll break you of sticking a gun in a man's face in the middle of the night."

"You ain't got no call to threaten me like that," he said, his voice kind of shaky.

"Oh, yes," I said quickly. "Yes, I do. I don't like you goddamn people. You understand that? I don't like you."

And now it had come time to do what I didn't think I could do. What I'd never done before. They were kind of spread out, just standing there with their hands in the air. Gaines was to my left and I advanced my horse until we were only about three feet apart. Chulo and Wilcey were watching me. I looked over at Wilcey. "You still say yes?"

He nodded and I swung back to Gaines. I said to him, "Gaines, I'm going to kill you."

He got that little thin-lipped smile on his face, which was about a half sneer. He said, "Maybe you are and maybe you ain't. That ain't been decided yet."

I shook my head. He didn't get it. "No," I said. "I'm going to kill you here and now, just as you are." I leveled my revolver down on him, holding it straight out from my shoulder.

It took him aback and the alarm registered on his face. "What's this?" he asked me. "Is this all the chance you going to give me?"

"Yes," I said. "Just about the same chance as you gave my partner, the Tinhorn. The gambler you killed in cold blood. That's the way I'm going to kill you."

"Now, wait a minute, Young," he said. "I never done no such. I don't care what you heard. He was armed."

"Cut the shit, Gaines," I said. "He could have had a Gatling gun and it wouldn't have done him no good with you. We both know that. He was nothing but a good-hearted small-time gambler who didn't know nothing about men like you and I. So you killed him. I doubt you had any other reason to kill him except you knew he was my partner and you'd done recognized me for what I was and you was scared I'd knock you out of being the big dog in the alley. Well, you made a mistake, Gaines."

"Listen, Young," he said, and his voice was getting a little strain in it. "Maybe what you say is right. Maybe I was trying to draw you out. But this ain't yore style. I've heard it ain't yore style. Give me a play and then do it."

"No," I said. And his words were cutting through me. "I know it ain't my style. And I feel pretty bad about it. But there it is. You made your mistake a week ago. And now you are going to pay for it. That was my good friend and I intend to serve you as you served him. Don't go out begging, Gaines. I don't like you, but I respect you."

He said, "I wouldn't beg you for the sweat off a hog's balls. You go to hell." And he put his hands down and started toward me.

I shot him square in the center of the chest and he went straight backward and fell in a heap and didn't move.

I looked at Wilcey. "Fair enough?"

"Damn straight," he said.

I raised up in my stirrups. "All right. You two." And I motioned at Sawyer and the other guard. "Get your boots off."

They were standing there goggle-eyed at what I'd just done. They didn't move.

I cocked my revolver again. "I said get them boots off and right now."

Sawyer said, "But our feet will freeze."

"Sawyer," I told him, "I don't give a fuck if you freeze all over. Get them boots off and do it now! I'm ready to shoot you."

Ormsby said, "You, whatever your name is, you are a murderer! I just saw you shoot my man down in cold blood!"

"Shut up," I told him, "or you may be next."

They sat down and started taking off their boots, Ormsby too. "No," I told him, "not you. You keep yours on."

Well, we were wasting too much time and I was starting to get a little worried. The road was staying clear, but for how much longer I could only guess.

When they had their boots off Wilcey took them and tied them on the horses we were going to turn loose after we'd dragged them out on the prairie a ways. The two barefoot men were hopping around already, their feet beginning to get mighty cold. I got off my horse and walked up to Ormsby. I had one more piece of business to do. I stuck my cocked revolver up to his ear and told him to pull his pants leg up.

"What?" he asked me, looking a little confused. "What?"

The cold wind was starting to get up a little more. Gaines was lying just a few feet from us. He looked awful dead. The front of his coat was beginning to show a few traces of blood seeping through.

"You heard me, motherfucker," I said. "Hitch up yore britches leg. The one near me."

He didn't understand what I was saying but he understood that cocked pistol in his ear. He did as he was told. I said, "Now, cant the top of your boot toward me and don't move."

He did it, his face all white and looking like he was too scared to breathe. With my free hand I unbuttoned my pants and took out my dong and pissed his boot full. The look on his face when I began was something to behold. It was shock about as pure and simple as you can get it. He wanted to move, but I shoved the end of my revolver against his ear and said, "Careful."

He froze. Behind me Chulo and Wilcey were laughing. I tell you, I ain't normally a mean man, but I meant to humiliate this stuffed shirt as bad as he'd humiliated a bunch of other men in the past. When I was finished I buttoned up my pants and then told him, "Now, then, you stupid sonofabitch. See if you can pour it out. The directions are on the heel."

Chulo and Wilcey were still laughing and the other two, between hopping around on their cold, bare feet, were staring at me slack-jawed.

I said, "Chulo!"

"Dígame, señor."

I said, "Hamstring him."

Chulo laughed. *"Con mucho gusto!"*

Ormsby was staring at me. "What? What did you tell him to do?"

"Hamstring you," I said.

Chulo was coming forward, his white teeth gleaming in his black face, taking out that big, sharp clasp knife of his.

This too wasn't my style, but I'd backed myself into a corner. I'd made the other two take off their boots for the purpose of delaying their walk into town. But I'd let Ormsby keep his for the purpose of showing him *my* contempt for him. Well, I couldn't very well leave him well shod so that he could make good time into town. That wouldn't have suited our purposes. So, after I'd done what I'd done out of vindictiveness I still had to go on being a professional at my trade and make it hard for him to walk. And hamstringing was the only thing I could think of right off the bat like that. I'd been hamstrung once before myself when a bullet had cut through the back of my thigh and, I tell you, it was a good six weeks before I could get around as well as could be expected.

Chulo was coming forward, that gleaming blade in his hand and Ormsby was walking backward, the piss in his boot squishing with every step. I took two steps forward and stuck the barrel of my revolver between his eyes. "Move one more inch and I'll blow your fucking brains out."

He stopped. He said, "You ain't civilized!"

"No," I said. "But you are. You build a fence and starve everybody out that's south of it. That's civilized?"

"That's business," he kind of whined.

"Well," I said. "This is my business. And if you believe business is business then you ain't got no kick coming. Just don't move."

Chulo was beside him and then his hand flashed and a thin line of red suddenly showed on the back of the thigh of Ormsby's fancy ripcord breeches. His leg gave and then he sat down.

"Might as well be comfortable," I told him. "You ain't going nowhere for a while."

His face was white and shocked. "I'll get you for this," he said. "I'll run you down."

"You better hope you don't," I said. I looked at my two partners. "Mount up."

We swung into the saddle and I leveled my revolver at Sawyer and the other guard. "Get on your faces."

They fell to the earth immediately. "Now," I said, "I can kill you now or I can kill you in the next hour if you move. Personally I'd like to kill you now. You figure you can lay here the better part of an hour before you start into town?"

They said, "Yes, sir!" in unison.

"Good," I said. I turned to my partners. "Let's git."

We put our horses into as good a gallop as we could manage, dragging the other five horses on lead. We took a kind of north by northeast angle, hoping our victims would mark on it and think we were heading for the Oklahoma territory. I kept glancing back, waiting to drop that buggy and the dead bodies out of sight over the horizon. Once I saw we had, I sang out to Wilcey, "Turn 'em loose!"—meaning the horses on lead.

And then we cut directly for the south. We were riding hard. We kept the horses in a hard gallop until they began to blow excessively hard and then I signaled my partners to pull them down. We came to a lope and then a trot and then a walk, just walking them, letting them have a blow.

Wasn't any of us singing and shouting, even though we had at least $10,000 in gold in our saddlebags. We all knew we had a ways to go before we could spend it.

And I was considerably troubled. More so by hamstringing Ormsby than by shooting Gaines, though the cold-blooded killing would weigh a long time in my mind.

I said to Wilcey, "I've come down considerably."

He said, "How so?"

We were walking along in the cold wind, leading our horses. Wilcey was walking between me and Chulo. "That that I did this morning," I said. "I ain't proud of it. I had figured out in my mind what I was going to do to Gaines, but I never knowed what I was going to do to Ormsby. It's kind of taken me off guard about myself."

Wilcey said, "Hell, forget it, Will. Don't you know that sonofabitch would have strung you up by yore thumbs and cut yore balls off if he'd had the chance? And you know Gaines had it coming. Hell, when you shot the bastard I was just wishing it was me doing it. Don't you turn your mind to it again."

And Chulo said, *"No importa, mi amigo. Es bueno. Es mucho bromar por un patron."*

A big joke on the boss.

Well, I reckon it was that and a little bit more.

"Fuck it," I said. "We got to make some tracks." We swung into the saddle. My responsibility was to my partners and the woman that was waiting for me. Not to some outlandish sense of pride that said you had to give even your worst enemies a fair shake.

The hell with that.

We pounded on, working the horses hard. They were ranch-company flesh, but we were goddamn well making them earn their pay. I reckoned it was about eight miles to old man Sutter's place and we kept the horses going after it most of the way. We finally raised his shack out of the horizon and come pounding into it, hell bent for leather.

True to his word, old man Sutter and his two boys were out front holding our horses. We came skidding to a stop, our horses lathered and blowing. Without a word we jumped to the ground and began jerking off saddles and bridles and saddlebags and transferring them to our fresh mounts.

Sutter said, "Be they close behind?"

"I don't think so," I said. "Not yet. But we got to make every second count. I had to kill two of them."

From where he was working at his horse Wilcey asked me, "How'd you arrange this, Will?"

"Didn't do my job for the company."

"Is that him?"

"Yes."

Wilcey laughed.

We were about ready to go. I told Sutter, "These horses we rode in on are ranch-company horses. You better drive 'em off. Or they'll probably wander."

"The boys'll rub 'em down. Don't ker whose stock they be, wouldn't turn no animal out in the cold lathered up as these be."

That's what I liked about Sutter. I reached in my saddlebags and got four twenty-dollar gold pieces to pay him the eighty dollars I still owed him. But he put his hands behind his back.

"No, sir! Nooooo, sir! You done gimme enough."

I didn't have time to argue with the old fool so I stuffed the money in the hand of one of his moon-faced boys. "Give that to your maw," I said.

Sutter started in to protest, but I was already swinging into the saddle. "Sutter," I said, "one more boon. If anybody comes asking, you ain't seen us. But you did see three horsemen going hell bent for leather heading north while you was out looking for some cattle this morning."

He nodded. "A safe journey to ye."

"Thanks. We got to get. Much obliged for all your help." Then we wheeled our horses and headed south at a gallop. I figured it was about thirty-five miles to Amarillo from where we were at and I intended to make it not too long after dark.

We rode hard, not overusing our horses, but keeping them at a steady pace. We would gallop for twenty or thirty minutes and then get off and walk, leading our horses and letting them take a blow. We didn't waste much breath talking. Occasionally one of us would get a bottle of whiskey out and we'd pass it back and forth as we walked. It was plenty cold, the wind straight out of the north and freshening.

Wilcey said, "I swear, I believe I've got a permanent chill in my bones. I don't think I'll ever get warm again. When we get to the border I'm going to lay down in the Rio Grande River and soak for four days."

But mostly we just made tracks, trying to put as much distance as we could between us and that Skillet Ranch country.

You'd have thought the cold would have bothered Chulo the most but, no, he just kept plodding along, every once in a while flashing those white teeth and laughing about something.

He was one tough *hombre*, I tell you.

After about three hours I called a quick halt so we could eat a little something. We squatted on the ground, holding our reins in our hands and eating some cold beef and biscuits and drinking whiskey.

Chulo said, "How much you figure, *amigo?*"

I shrugged. "Better 'n ten thousand," I said. "Your share will keep you in tamales for a while, greaser."

They vaguely knew our plans, mostly just knowing

we were heading for the border, but not exactly where. Wilcey said, "You figured out for sure where we're heading?"

I nodded. "Going to Del Rio first. Very little law there. After that we may wander down to Laredo. First thing we're going to do is get across the border and lay around Mexico for a time. Spend a little of this money."

I guess Wilcey and I both thought of the same thing at the same time, for he said, "Wish the old preacher man was along to spend some of it."

"Yeah," I said. "Well." I put my gloves back on. "Let's get moving."

We went hard after it for another two hours. At one point Wilcey said, "Will, you seem to pointin' us awful close to Amarillo. Hadn't we better shy off east a little?"

I didn't say anything. I still hadn't told him or Chulo about Hester and about the fact that I was going to have to make a quick trip into Amarillo. The main reason I hadn't told them was because I was dreading it. They wouldn't like it one damn bit and I couldn't blame them. Wilcey was the one I was really worried about. Chulo, after a minute or two, would just shrug and say, *"No importa."* But Wilcey was going to be mad as hell.

Well, I knew I couldn't put it off much longer. We went on for another hour and, as the sun was starting to get low in the sky, I called another halt.

After we'd had a few bites to eat I told them what I was going to do. Wilcey immediately blew sky-high. He said, "Will, have you lost your goddamn mind? You can't go into Amarillo!"

I explained I was just going to take her some money and make sure she could get a train. "Listen," I said, "I won't be more than a half an hour. Forty-five minutes at the most."

He said, "You ain't talking with your head, you are talking with your ass. Here we just pulled off one hell of a robbery and you going to mess it up over some goddamn woman! Goddamn, this just about takes the cake!"

"Will you wait a minute. I'm just going in to the train depot and come straight back. Ain't nobody going to see me. And so what if they do? They ain't got the word out that fast."

"Damnit, Wilson, you know you never had no luck with women. You say so yourself. And here you are going to go in and git your dumb ass killed over another one. When are you going to learn?" He turned to the black Mexican. "Chulo, talk some sense to him."

But Chulo just shook his head and showed his white teeth. "Where the weemen are concerned this *chumacho* don't got no sense. He is *hombre muy estúpido.*"

"Ah, shit!" Wilcey said. He got up and stalked a few feet away, cussing a blue streak.

"Look," I said, "Ya'll can go on without me. I'll catch up."

"Bullshit on that!" Wilcey said. "We don't do it that way and we ain't going to start now. But tell me one thing: What the hell you going to do with that goddamn woman?"

"Marry her," I said.

"And then what? She going to live down on the border with you? What you going to do, start you a farm?"

"No, Wilcey," I said wearily, "I'm going to go on making my living the only way I know how. Just like I been doing before." He had a certain amount of say coming and I was willing he should have it, but I hoped he wouldn't go too far.

"Then what?" he asked me. "Where ya'll going to set up housekeeping? In jail? On the dodge? I mean, can she make pretty good biscuits on the back of a running horse?"

"That's enough, Wilcey," I said.

"No, it ain't. It ain't near enough. Somebody's got to make you see some sense, damnit! Same thing going to happen to you happened to a lot of men who tried to be married outlaws. You'll have her set up in a house somewheres and you'll be slippin' back to see her. Only one night the law will be waiting and then Chulo and I had better get our black suits out."

"Enough, I said! Now, mount up. You had your say. Now, let it lie." They saw I meant it and they got on their horses and we started on.

It commenced to get dark, which was a good thing for, after we'd ridden on for about another hour, we could see the lights of Amarillo reflected against the dark sky. No one said a word as I led us to a point about a mile east of Amarillo. They pulled up as I did and I said, "Now, look, I'm going on in. Ya'll can do what you want to. If you want to go on I'll catch up."

Chulo said, "No, *amigo,* I wait."

And Wilcey said, "I done told you how I feel. Go on and make a goddamn fool of yourself, but be quick about it."

"All right," I said. "Ya'll get down and rest your horses. If I ain't back in an hour go on without me." I reached around and untied the saddlebags that had my share of the gold in it and pitched it across the rump of Wilcey's horse. "Hang on to this for me," I said. Then I touched spurs to my horse and started toward Amarillo.

Chapter Nine

I picked my way carefully through the outskirts of the town. I had a pretty good idea where the train depot was, having noted it when we'd come through heading north.

It was good and dark and there weren't many people on the streets on the side of town I was going through. I struck the tracks and then turned north and came up on the depot right at the outskirts of town. The wind was whipping up just as the moon began to rise. I stopped my horse at the depot and dismounted and tied him. I tried to see in through the windows to see if she was in there, but they were too fogged up.

Finally I just opened the door and looked inside. She was sitting on one of those benches with the iron armrests. She looked up just as I stepped through the door.

"Oh, Wilson!" she said loudly, her face lighting up.

I wished she weren't so free with my name, but I suppose it didn't matter. Outside of her the only other one in the station was the ticket agent in behind his little teller's cage grille.

I hugged her briefly when she came up and then led her back to the bench and sat down.

"Oh, Will," she said, "I'm so glad to see you. I've been so worried."

"All right, all right. Did you have any trouble?"

"No. But it just be so far and so cold. And I was

a-wishin' you were there." She looked at me. "Be ye all right?"

"Yes," I said.

"Are you hurt?"

"No, now hush."

"Did you do murder?"

"Sssh," I said sharply. I glanced around. The ticket agent was at his window watching us. "Listen, what about the train? What did you find out about going south?"

"I kin get to Austin, but it'll be tomorrow afternoon. Then I go on from there."

"All right," I said. "We need to get you to a hotel. Go and ask the agent where there's a hotel right close by. And don't waste any time. I've got to hurry."

She got up and went to the window and spoke briefly to the agent. I noticed him glancing over her shoulder at me while they talked. When she came back she said he'd told her there was a little hotel just a block up the street.

"Com'on," I said. I picked up her one bag. The rest of her stuff was lying over in the corner. I pointed to it and asked the agent, "Be all right to leave that here overnight?"

"Be fine," he said.

Carrying her bag I helped her out the door and we started up the street. She looked a little travel-worn, but other than that she seemed all right.

She said, "You don't seem very glad to see me."

"I am," I told her. "But, goddamn, Hester, I've just robbed and killed two men today and then ridden like hell for forty miles. I ain't really able to show how I feel right now."

She was hugging onto my arm with both of hers. Well, that was all right. She'd done a mighty brave thing leaving all she had and coming away with me on nothing more than my word.

And me a robber and a killer at that.

We went in the hotel and I got her a room. The clerk gave me a key and we went on upstairs. I told her, once we were inside, that I couldn't stay long. "My two partners are waiting and I got to get back as quick as I can."

She sat down on the bed and looked up at me. "Don't you even have time to—I mean, couldn't you stay long enough—"

"No," I said. I walked over to the window and looked out. Her room was right on the front of the hotel and the sloping roof over the porch was just below her window. "Oh, here," I said. I got a hundred dollars out of my pocket and put it on the bureau. "There's your money to get to Del Rio on. Now, remember, the Cattleman's Hotel. And use your regular name there and don't mention mine to anyone."

"Yes," she said.

I went over and picked her up in my arms and kissed her. I didn't feel much like kissing her right then, but it had nothing to do with her. She clung to me hard. Hell, I knew she was scared and in a strange place. I tried to reassure her. "Hester, it'll be all right. You'll have a nice train ride and then I'll be along before you know it. You'll see. It'll all work out."

"Is Mister Sutter looking out for my stock?"

"Yes," I said. I patted her back. "But you're not going to need that stock anymore. We'll get married as soon as I get to Del Rio and we'll have plenty of money. We got over ten thousand dollars this morning."

It tickled me to see her hand go to her mouth and her eyes get a shocked look. "You be joshing me," she said.

I shook my head. "No, I'm not."

"My lands!" she said. "I never reckoned they was that much money in all of the United States!"

"There is," I said. "And we'll have plenty."

I was about to kiss her again when there came a sudden pounding at the door. A voice called, "Wilson Young! This is the law! Open this door!"

Hester grabbed my arm and clung. She said, "Oh, Wilson!"

I didn't blame her for it. She didn't know any better. She didn't do it on purpose, but she'd done it and now the fat was in the fire. They couldn't have been sure before, but now they were.

I tried to jerk loose from her, knowing what was coming. She was holding my right arm and I couldn't draw my gun. Just as I succeeded in flinging her away from me the door opened and the guns began to boom. As I drew I felt a blow hit me in the left shoulder. I staggered toward the window, firing as fast as I could. The room was so full of smoke I couldn't see a thing. A bullet broke the window out behind me and then I crashed through it backward, landing on the porch roof and rolling to the edge and then dropping off. I hit wrong and I felt a sharp pain in my ankle, but I was up and running before they could get to the window and fire at me.

I ran, limping a little, to the train station, jumped on my horse and wheeled around, firing at the ticket agent inside the depot so he would duck and not see which way I was headed. I was satisfied that it was him who'd been wired to be on the lookout for me and had called the law.

But I had no time for thinking. I was dashing through the dark back streets of the town, and then onto the open prairie. I knew I'd been shot, but it wasn't hurting much. I felt a little weak and my left arm was feeling numb, but, other than that, I felt fine.

I pointed my horse for where I'd left my partners and pretty soon I made out their dark humps in the night. I never slowed my pace as I approached and they must have figured I was on the run for they were mounted and in a gallop by the time I came up to them.

We didn't say a word, just laid on the spurs and tore south as fast as we could go. It would take them some time to organize a catch party and I intended to be plenty far away from there by then.

I only knew one thing. I might have $10,000 in gold, but I was womanless again. Hester would get me killed before she learned to be an outlaw's wife.

Chapter Ten

It was a good many days riding before I would talk about what had happened. Chulo and Wilcey could see I was low in my mind so they just left me alone.

The gunshot wound hadn't amounted to much. The bullet had broken my left collarbone and then gone on out, leaving a clean hole. I'd dosed it up with whiskey and then we'd taken a piece of rope and bound my left arm tight to my side so as to keep the bone from moving around while it knitted. It wasn't much bother except when I tried to sleep. I'd had a collarbone broken before and I didn't pay much attention to it.

But the hurt about Hester was something else again. I'd made a lot of plans that had included her and to see them go aglimmering was a painful matter indeed.

Finally, about four or five days down the road from Amarillo, we were camped near the little town of Mason, west of Austin. Chulo had gone in and got us some whiskey and we were sitting around in the sunshine, beginning to feel we were getting back to God's country, and taking a little rest from the hard pace we'd been setting ever since I'd come dashing out of Amarillo.

We'd taken the saddles off our horses and were letting their backs air out a little. We were just sitting around on the ground, not saying much of anything.

We were all kind of weary from all the days of hard riding. Fortunately we hadn't had any trouble to speak of. But then we'd stayed away from the towns, just approaching one every now and then so Wilcey or Chulo could go in for supplies and whiskey. I reckoned we hadn't seen five people all told on the trip, and those just at a passing distance.

It was a warm day and we were sitting there enjoying it. Wilcey said, "Boy, this sun feels good. I about thought that big coat was part of my skin. Pass me that whiskey, Chulo."

He took a pull and then offered me the bottle. I had a slug and then kind of stared off. I knew my partners were wondering what had happened. Well, I didn't blame them. So was I. I said, kind of like I was thinking outloud, "A man that's in the kind of business I'm in needs a woman that's near as quick as he is. You ain't quick in this business, you'll get killed. And Hester wasn't quick enough."

They didn't say anything for a moment and then Wilcey asked me, kind of gentle, "She going to meet you in Del Rio?"

I shook my head. "Won't matter if she does. We ain't going to Del Rio. And even if we was it still wouldn't matter. She done some wrong things back there in a hotel room in Amarillo. I know she didn't go to do 'em. I know she didn't know no better. But it still don't make no difference. It convinced me she wouldn't make a wife for the likes of me. She been used to leading another kind of life and mine's too different. By the time she learned what to do it'd be too late. She'd of gotten me killed."

"Was that the shooting we heard?"

"Yeah," I said. "With the law at the door she said my name. She just plain got scared and lost her head. But it don't matter the reason. Like I say, she's been used to a far different kind of life than the life she'd lead with me. I'm going to miss her. She was a sweet woman. But it can't be helped. Now, let's say no more about the matter."

Wilcey said, "If not Del Rio, where we headed?"

"Straight for Laredo," I said.

"Hell, that's only about a four-or-five-day ride from here. We'll get there in good shape."

"Yes. And then we'll go across the border and have us a little good times. Spend some of this goddamn cold-ass money." We'd counted our take and we'd come away with $11,025, which we thought was a respectable showing.

"Reckon they'll be looking for us on the border?"

"Of course," I said. "But we ain't going to stay on the border. We're going on into the interior of Mexico for awhile. Let things cool down a little."

Wilcey laughed. "I bet that Ormsby don't cool down for a time. I bet he stays plenty angry."

"Let him," I said. "One more wanted notice either way ain't going to make no difference."

Chulo was grinning big. He said, "Mexico. *Estoy bueno.*"

"Yes, Mexico, you damn greaser. I got to get you out of Texas before you accidently hurt somebody. 'Course somebody could get their eyes hurt just looking at you."

He held up one finger and I knew what was coming. "I like to rob one Mexican bank."

"Hell with that," I said. "Let's rob us a whole bunch of Mexican banks and get rich and live like dons." I got up. "Let's move," I said. "I want to get home." I was already feeling better, just thinking about it.